Malvan Born

by

Nancy Scharding

For information on the author's other novels, visit her website at:

www. LimberlostBooks.com

ISBN: 978-1-939667-02-1

For my son, Michael, who encouraged me to write a book

How fast has brother followed brother, from sunshine to the sunless land.

~*William Wordsworth (1770-1850)*

CONTENTS

1

THE DELIVERY

Hearing the sylvan's knock, the old servant got up heavily from the hearth, cinched her belt tighter around her waist, and shuffled to the balcony door, her slippers flip-flopping, her robe hiked up in the back, the front hem dragging on the floor. Even during this hectic evening, she'd been half-watching, half-listening for Logos. Two weeks ago, she'd found a feather jammed under her door. However, half of the time she found a feather, Logos never came. He never explained why not, and she never asked.

She flung open the door to find the sylvan soaked, his wet hair trailing down over his forehead, water dripping off his elbows and wings. Her eyes widened. He had two babies in his arms.

"Twins!" she exclaimed. She stood at the open door speechless for a few moments before speaking. "Come in, Lord Logos," she said, stepping aside to let him enter.

"Good evening, mistress Neela," he replied, as polite and self-composed as usual in spite of his bedraggled appearance.

Neela snorted. "Not so good, Lord Logos. This weather is awful, and Lady Huntley's gone into labor—early again. I just came in to make her some medicine—why, you're soaked! Come dry yourself by the fire." She frowned at the babies. "Twins," she repeated. "I can't place two. One will have to go to the children's asylum, poor little thing."

Seeing that his wings were dripping water on the floor, Logos snapped a wing forward and down, flinging the water towards the fireplace, and making the coals sizzle and throwing the scent of wet ashes into the room. Turning around, he cleared his other wing. Then he lowered one of the babies onto the bed.

Neela bent down over the child. "Poor thing must be soaked to the skin." She removed the thin gold blanket to inspect the baby. "Well, I'll be—he's perfectly dry. How could that be?"

"Our fabric is so closely woven that it's almost watertight," Logos explained. "And I had him tucked under my tunic. But he's probably chilled."

Pulling her shawl from the chair, Neela wrapped the baby in it. "He's very small, but he's a fine boy. I shouldn't have any trouble placin' him." She took the child's hand, and he grasped her finger. Neela examined his hand. "What's this odd mark between his finger and thumb? It looks almost like a bite."

Logos looked down. "It's nothing—just a birthmark."

Neela scoffed. "Let me see the other one," she said, snatching the child from his arms. It was bound in a narrow, elaborately decorated fabric which she recognized as Logos' head covering. She unwrapped the tiny baby.

"Oh," she gasped, almost dropping the infant. "It's deformed." The child's chest was thick, front to back, with a prominent sternum, and on its back were two feathered knobs.

"He's *not* deformed," said Logos, grabbing the child back. "He's a sylvan. He belongs to me—I mean—he's going home with me."

"Let me wrap him up in a nice, warm blanket."

"I'll take care of him." Logos re-wrapped the baby in his head gear and snuggled him to his chest. "This will do fine."

A loud shout from the hall interrupted them. A man's deep voice bellowed, "Neela, where are you. Come at once!"

Neela jumped. "The Master! I have to go. I'm sorry. I can't stay and visit."

"That's all right. I need to get back before the storm gets any worse. Goodbye for now."

With that, Logos strode to the door and opened it, letting in a fresh blast of cold air and rain. He sprang onto the railing, opened his wings, jumped into the air and was gone, sending a tremendous downdraft that rattled the door on its hinges.

Neela stood by the door, gaping into the sky. Although she had watched Logos take flight many times, she never ceased to be amazed at the sight. She had to push hard to shut the door. The wind was definitely getting stronger. She hoped Logos would be all right.

"Neela!"

She turned as Lord Huntley walked into her room without knocking. "What's keeping you," he shouted. "We need you—oh!" He stopped when he saw the baby lying on her bed. "Oh yes, of course, you have a baby for adoption. I didn't hear anybody come to the front door, though."

Neela walked over to the fireplace. "I came back to make some tea for Lady Huntley. I thought maybe the herbs might help stop the contractions." She swung a metal hook out from over the fire and lifted the iron kettle off with a folded up towel. Then she poured the thick, strong-smelling liquid into a tin cup and took a sip. "It's done."

"Very good," Lord Huntley said. "But can't you make tea without getting water all over the floor?"

"Yes, Mi'Lord." Neela could have cried with relief. He hadn't seen Logos. As she followed Lord Huntley back to his bedroom, she thought what a narrow escape they had

had. She must remember to lock her door next time Logos showed up. And what a shame Logos had to leave. She wanted to talk to him. Although he would never tell her where the babies came from, only that their parents couldn't keep them and that they needed a home, sometimes he dropped hints about his life. She wanted to ask why he brought a sylvan baby with him—in a storm no less. And she wanted to know when its wings would open. She set the thoughts aside as she entered Lord Huntley's bedroom.

Lady Huntley was too weak to sit up. Neela propped up some pillows underneath, the woman's head, so she could sip the tea. The desperate woman grabbed onto the hot cup with both hands, bravely gulping down the foul-smelling brew.

Neela prayed the herbs would help. The baby was coming early—like all the other babies her Lady had lost.

Lady Huntley finished her drink with an involuntary shudder and handed her the cup. "Oh, Neela, I cannot lose this one. It will be my last."

Neela searched for the right words. "Take courage, Letty," she said, lapsing into the familiar nickname she had called her Lady when she had been a girl. "I'll do my best. The tea should help you. Lie down now and try to get some rest …"

"We won't lose it," Lord Huntley interrupted. "Everything will be all right, I promise you, Leutha."

Neela stared at him in shock. How dare he promise such a thing? She hoped to God he was right, but she feared he was wrong. For a while, Lady Huntley rested, and Neela began to hope. Perhaps the tea had helped. But soon the relentless contractions started again, stronger than before. Lady Huntley began to sob, helplessly.

"Is there nothing else we can do, Neela?" pleaded Lord Huntley, his voice breaking. Neela had never seen the Master this distraught. He was always so confident, so arrogant, so much in charge of everything.

"Is there any ice left, Mi'Lord?" Neela asked.

"How would I know? Perhaps, there are a few pieces under the straw."

"Get it for me." The words felt strange coming out of her mouth. She was not used to giving the Master orders, but he didn't seem to notice. As though happy to have something constructive to do, he ran to the hallway and barked commands at the group of frightened servants huddled outside the door. One of them shot off down the hall. Surprisingly soon, the young servant, drenched from the rain and out of breath, arrived with a chunk of dirty ice, plastered with straw. Without cleaning it off, Neela wrapped the ice in a towel and laid it on Lady Huntley's swollen abdomen.

"Perhaps the cold will slow down the contractions," she said, although she had no hope left. Lady Huntley was fully dilated. The child would come shortly, save a miracle.

It soon became apparent that no miracle was to be had. Each contraction came closer together than the last, leaving Lady Huntley more exhausted. Lord Huntley paced the room, alternately wringing his hands and mopping his brow. His wife reached out to him. He knelt at her side and took her hand. "It'll be all right, Leutha, this one will survive, I promise you," he said again.

Neela glared at him. He was only trying to calm his wife, but how wrong to get her hopes up. She pressed her lips together to stay silent.

One more strong contraction and the baby emerged, along with way too much blood. It was a boy child, perfectly formed, but pale and motionless. Lady Huntley lost consciousness, and her eyes rolled up into her head. Lord Huntley turned to Neela, his scar livid against his pale face, his dark eyes wild. "My son must live. You must save him, Neela."

Neela carried the infant to her room. It would be better if her Lady never saw her baby, never held it. She laid the little waxen thing on her bed, cleaned out its mouth and nose, and massaged its hands and legs and chest. "Please, God, let this baby live. Sweet mother, let him live," she prayed over and over. But the child did not breathe. Neela stopped and mopped the sweat from her brow.

She turned to find Lord Huntley watching her, leaning against the door for support, so pale she expected him to faint. He opened his mouth to speak, but for a long time, nothing came out. "It's dead, isn't it?" he asked in a strange, choked voice.

"Yes, Mi'Lord," she answered softly. "It never took a single breath."

Lord Huntley looked utterly defeated. In the next room, Lady Huntley regained consciousness and called out. "Where's my baby? I want my baby. Arthur, where are you?"

Just then, the foundling that Logos had left began to whimper. Lord Huntley looked up and whispered hoarsely, "It's alive!"

"No, Mi'Lord," Neela said quickly. "That's only the orphan child."

Lord Huntley's eyes darted to the baby. He crossed the room with quick strides. "What is it—boy or girl?"

"A boy, Mi'Lord."

"Healthy?"

"Yes, Mi'Lord. He seems to be."

Lord Huntley leaned down and examined the baby. "He has an injury on his hand, but otherwise he's perfect. In fact, he has dark hair and eyes, like me. He'll do," he declared. He scooped up the baby and headed for the door. Suddenly realizing where he was going, Neela grabbed his arm. "What are you doing?"

He shook her arm off. "I'm switching the babies."

2

THE STORM

Logos quickly tried to gain altitude. He wasn't worried about being seen—the darkness of the night would hide him—but he needed to find an updraft, so he could glide and rest his weary wings. The lightweight baby in his arms was no burden at all, but he had already made two flights that day, and he was flying directly into a head wind. He wasn't trained to be a long-distance flyer, so he had never developed the necessary muscles. His outer garments were already soaked, and the rain settled on his wings, adding to the weight he carried. He snapped his wings downward, flinging the water off, but it soon built up again.

A sylvan does not admit to fatigue. His old teacher's voice came unbidden into his head. He would distract himself by thinking of Tamara. He smiled. He still couldn't believe he had won her. It was no secret that her parents didn't trust him because he was malvan-born. In their eyes, Tomos, Captain of the Guards, the strongest flyer in the Colony of New Solari, and from a pure sylvan family, would be a much more suitable match. From childhood, both Tamara's and Tomos' parents had expected their children to marry, so they had become engaged. And then Tamara had met Logos and broken off the engagement. Somehow—he thanked the Goddess for the miracle—Tamara loved him, not Tomos.

Logos hadn't intended to fall in love, and being malvan born, he certainly never expected to find anyone who would marry him. But when he had met Tamara last summer at the annual Blessing Day ceremony, he had fallen hopelessly in love. Growing up without parents, he hadn't known it was possible to love someone so much. Tamara was the only person he'd shared his secret with—a secret that could lose him his position if it became known—that he had been working with a human. *A sylvan must not have any contact with humans.*

Neela. He chuckled at the thought of the sensible old servant, now his friend. Handing over the human baby to her had been such a relief. She would find the boy a loving home. Years ago, when he had just become caretaker to the malvans, he had hated dropping off helpless babies in the back of a cold, dark church, not knowing how long it would be before they were found, or what would happen to them. He remembered the night he met Neela. That was the first time he had ever come in contact with a human. How they had both jumped when they saw each other—he certain she would scream and expose him—she (as she later told him) afraid the Angel of Death had come to fetch her.

After the initial fright, Logos had backed hastily toward the doorway to escape. To his surprise, the human quickly regained her composure and blocked his path. "That's a baby, isn't it?" she said, pointing to the basket in the pew. "Where did you get it?" She wagged her finger in his face and asked, "You stole it, didn't you?"

Logos, taken aback by her bad manners as much as by the verbal barrage—*A sylvan does not point*—stared at her. Not knowing which question to answer first, he started with the first. "Yes, it's a baby—but I didn't steal it. Sylvans never steal."

"What's a sylvan?" asked Neela.

What a stupid question, Logos thought, and then realized it wasn't. Humans weren't even aware that sylvans existed. "Sylvans are winged people, like me," he explained.

"You're not an angel then?"

Now it was Logos' turn to be puzzled. "What's an angel?"

"A messenger from God Almighty, like them." Neela pointed at one of the marble statues beside the altar. "With wings, like yours—only, real beings, not statues."

"I know nothing of angels. I am a sylvan, from the original race."

Still looking confused, Neela asked, "What is your name?"

"I am called Logos."

"My name is Neela." She circled back to the subject. "Is it an orphan?"

"Not exactly, Ue-Mem Neela, but its parents are unable to care for it. It has no home."

"Can I have it then? I know someone who will give it a good home."

"It's yours." He walked around her to leave.

"Wait, Mi'Lord. It's you who's been droppin' off babies here all along. Isn't it?"

"It is."

"Where do you get them?"

"I told you. I cannot say, Ue-Mem Neela."

"You take a big chance of being seen or caught."

"That is true."

"Might I be so bold as to ask somethin' of you?"

"Ask," he said, wondering what this curious person could possibly want from him.

"Could you bring the babies to me at the Manor House?"

"You can find homes for more babies?"

"I'm a midwife. I always know who wants a child. I have found good homes for all the babes the priests brung me."

Logos thought for a moment. Why not? Obviously, that would be a better arrangement for the babies. True, his training had taught him to avoid humans at all cost, but he couldn't see any harm in this little person, and it would be nice not to have to sneak in the church and leave a baby here unattended. He did risk being discovered. "How would I get them to you?" he asked.

"I live in the Manor House outside the village. It's the biggest house around. My room is on the north side, overlookin' the forest. There ain't no other buildings there, so nobody would see you come and go, especially if you came at evening time. I'm on the second floor. There is a small balcony where you can land."

Logos had been studying her as she spoke. He could feel the goodness and honesty radiating from her. He knew instinctively that he could trust her. He made his decision.

"That sounds quite convenient. I shall do that in the future." He bowed formally, backed out the door, turned and disappeared into the night before she could ask any more questions.

Over the years, the arrangement had worked well for all concerned. He jammed a feather under Neela's door when a baby might be coming, and she scouted for parents. The adoptive parents were happy to take a healthy baby and not ask any questions. And he and Neela had even become friends. They had learned much from each other, and ...

A gust of wind knocked him sideways, bringing him out of his reverie. He took his bearings with his eye rings, realized he had gained very little altitude and he had blown far off course. His wing joints had begun to ache—*A sylvan does not admit to pain*—but he was so tired of fighting the wind and not making any progress. The infant whimpered. He pulled its wrappings closer and blew warm air on its face. If the child got wet, it would get chilled. He should take shelter until the storm abated.

He circled, looking for a place to land. A lightning flash revealed an opening below. He flew lower to check the area out, waited for another flash of lightning to make sure it wasn't a river, and then threw his wings forward into gliding position, descended and landed on a narrow pathway. It wasn't natural, must be a human-made path. He took shelter under a large tree, shook the water from his wings and leaned against the tree.

The infant woke up and began a high-pitched keening. Logos pulled up the makeshift blanket to cover the child's head. "Hush, child. A sylvan does not cry," he said gently. Its crying subsided for a while, as though it understood him, and then began again. "You must be hungry. Well, I can't do anything about that right now."

The sun wasn't out, so they couldn't feed from the Goddess' life-giving rays. When he got home, Tamara would find a sylvana to breast-feed it until the sun came out. Then she would see to it that it got plenty of sunshine. The thought of Tamara cheered him: She would be waiting for him to see if he brought home an infant. She and the other sylvanas who worked on the children's platform would take turns caring for the child until someone was chosen to adopt it.

How good it would be to be home, to see Tamara again.

He rocked the baby until it quieted. Soon, they both fell asleep. From time to time, an occasional flash of lightning and clap of thunder briefly awakened him, but he never heard the crack of the branch that broke and knocked him unconscious, spilling the infant from his arms.

3

THE BURIAL

"Switch the babies?" Neela, unbelieving, stumbled along after Lord Huntley. "You can't do that."

He wheeled around. "I can and I am. For God's sake, woman, be quiet!"

The baby began to cry. Lord Huntley continued down the hall, Neela making little "*tsk-tsk*" noises behind him. Opening his bedroom door, he turned and hissed, "Silence!" He walked to the bed and lowered the squalling infant into his wife's arms. "Here he is, Leutha. Here's your son."

Lady Huntley was so weak, he had to help hold the baby to her side, but she kissed its cheek and stroked its downy head, laughing and crying at the same time. When she looked up at her husband, her smile was radiant. Years seemed to fall from her face.

"I'd like to name him Leuthur," she said, "from our names, Leutha and Arthur."

"That will be fine," Lord Huntley replied. Neela sniffed. She thought the name sounded like "Lucifer."

Lady Huntley closed her eyes, and her hands fell from the baby.

"Neela!" Lord Huntley shouted.

Neela turned her attention to saving the woman. She massaged her abdomen until the placenta passed. Her efforts were rewarded when the blood flow stopped, and Lady Huntley woke up again, asking for her baby. Neela handed the child to her, and then stood up and shot a questioning glance at Lord Huntley, who mouthed, "LA-TER."

To cover her distress, Neela bustled about being helpful. She brought fresh bedding, changed the bed, washed her Lady's face and found cotton swaddling for the baby. Finally, she excused herself to go to the kitchen on the excuse of getting some broth. She took the back door to avoid the group of servants in the hall. They had heard the baby cry and were talking excitedly. Word had already spread to the kitchen staff, too. The servants surrounded her, and peppered her with questions. "It's alive! Is it a boy or a girl? Is Lady Huntley all right?"

Neela pasted a smile on her face and forced herself to answer their questions. "They have a beautiful baby boy— small, about six pounds. Lady Huntley is weak, but she'll be fine." She escaped as soon as she could, explaining that she needed to take some food to Lady Huntley.

Neela brought in a bowl of broth and set it by the bedside. "Let me have the baby," she said, reaching for him, but Lady Huntley clung to him and held him closer. "No!" she shouted.

"Awright," Neela said, not wanting to upset her. "Will you take some broth for me, Letty?" she asked, coaxing her as she had when her Lady was a child.

Lady Huntley let herself be spoon-fed, opening her mouth dutifully like a baby bird. After she had swallowed most of the warm broth, the exhausted woman fell into a deep sleep, the infant still clutched to her side.

Lord Huntley stood beside her for a while watching her breathe. Satisfied that she was all right, he went to the door and addressed the waiting servants. "It's a boy," he said with a forced smile. "Mother and baby are doing well."

They cheered and shouted, "Congratulations, Mi'Lord."

"Thank you. You may celebrate by opening a barrel of beer from the cellar." More cheers went up, and the servants hurried off.

As Lord Huntley turned back to the waiting Neela, his smile disappeared. "We'll talk in your room."

She followed him silently into her room, and he closed the door behind them. They both stared at the little ashen form on Neela's bed. Neela glanced up at Lord Huntley reproachfully.

"I had to do it, Neela. Leutha would have gone mad if she lost this one—you know it's our last. She'll soon be forty-six."

Neela bowed her head. She had watched the master and his wife bury one small casket after another in the chapel. Lady Huntley had refused to let her babies be buried in the cold, stark graveyard, so Lord Huntley had a shallow crypt dug underneath the chapel floor. After each burial, Lady Huntley had spent more and more time in the chapel, crying and praying to have another child. A year ago, when her last baby died, they found her kneeling on the grave, rocking back and forth, and singing lullabies. Neela had coaxed her away, much worried about her state of mind.

"Yes," Neela said reluctantly, "Mayhap this is best for Lady Huntley, but what about your baby?"

"Prepare the body for burial," Lord Huntley ordered, "and bring it to the chapel. I'll meet you there." He left, pulling the door shut hard.

Neela, alone with the infant, said softly, "Lord, help me. It just ain't right to bury this child, unnamed and without a proper funeral." She reached for a pitcher of water and washed the blood and mucus from the body. As she set the pitcher down, she remembered Father Joseph saying that any Christian could baptize in an emergency. She took a crucifix from the wall, ignoring the nail, which clattered to the floor, and placed the cross on the baby's chest. Reaching for the pitcher again, she poured water on the baby's head and said, "Arthur Huntley, the Third, I baptize you in the name of the Father, and of the Son, and of the Holy Spirit."

When she had finished, she felt a little better. At least the baby was baptized. Now it could go to Heaven. She picked up the nail from the floor to place it back in the wall, and then stopped. Although barely literate, she knew her letters and a few words. Using the nail, she scratched a simple inscription on the back of the crucifix. She wrapped the body in the golden blanket Logos had brought the baby in, and tucked the crucifix inside.

Sounds of celebration arose from downstairs. Apparently, the barrel had been opened. Neela put on her heavy, wool cloak and sneaked down the back stairs, hiding the small bundle under her cloak. "Dear God, please don't let anyone see me now," she prayed. Her prayer was answered. No one entered the stairwell. She breathed a sigh of relief. No one had seen her.

When Neela entered the chapel, Lord Huntley was already there. He had pried open the marble slab covering the graves of his previous stillborn children and opened one of the caskets. The slab and the lid to the casket lay on the chapel floor. He got to his feet, closed the door and barred it. Taking the baby's body from Neela's arms, he carried it to the gaping hole, placed it in the casket on top of the bones of another child, and replaced the lid. He gazed on the casket for a moment, and then pulled the slab over the hole. It slid into place with a loud thud that echoed around the room and made Neela jump. The gravesite looked like it had never been disturbed.

Lord Huntley wiped the dust off his hands, picked up the Mass book from the altar and walked back to Neela. "Swear you'll never tell this to anyone."

Neela trembled. It was a fearful oath to swear, but she had no choice. Placing her shaking hand on the book, she said in a quavering voice, "I swear it, Mi'Lord."

"Very good," he said. "We will never speak of this again. Now go stay with my wife and son. And try to smile. You look like the Angel of Death itself."

4

THE RESCUE

Three of Lord Benefield's men were returning late to Benefield Manor from a wedding. Cooper, the youngest, had been elected to dismount and lead the way with a lantern shining a feeble ring of light on the muddy path. Smitty and Beeks rode behind him, single file with Smitty bringing up the rear. Smitty pulled his hat down over his ears. The talkative Beeks quit making lame jokes about the weather and grew silent. All three were dreaming about home—all they wanted was a warm fire, dry clothes, and a warm bed. The oilcloth ponchos they wore couldn't keep out the persistent, cold rain, which had worked its way down their necks and soaked them to the skin.

Smitty and Beek's horses, probably remembering snug stalls with sweet-smelling hay, had to be continually reined in to keep from riding over Cooper. The normal *clip-clop* of their hooves had been muted to a sodden *slosh-slosh*. Cooper, afraid he was lost, was anxiously looking for trail markers. He wouldn't admit it aloud, but he thought they should drop their reins and give the horses their heads. They knew the way home better than he did.

"*Ma-ouw!*"

The sound stopped Cooper in his tracks. The others reined up behind him. Cooper felt the hair rise at the back of his neck. A cat? No self-respecting cat would be out in this kind of weather. He swung the lantern over to the side of the path. "Hold up, men!"

"What is it, Cooper?"

"I see something. I think it's a body." He moved closer. "Oh, my God!"

"What is it?" Beeks and Smitty asked.

"It's—it's some sort of angel."

Hoots of laughter rang out. "Angel? Cooper, you must be nipping the rum on the sly. No wonder you can't find the way home."

Cooper ignored the teasing. "Get over here and take a look at this."

The two dismounted, still laughing. They followed the light to where Cooper's lantern shone down on the creature. Their jaws dropped open. "Gawd Almighty," Beeks said. "It *is* an angel. Is he alive?"

Cooper put his hand on the creature's chest and felt it rise. "He's still breathing. Help me lift this tree limb off him."

Cooper and Beeks grabbed the limb and lifted it off to one side. They kneeled down and peered at the injured creature. His short, blond hair was caked with blood, and one wing was bent backwards at an odd angle. Cooper whistled and said, "Look at those chest and shoulder muscles! He's hurt bad, and it looks like one of his wings is broken."

"What are we going to do with him?" Beeks asked Smitty.

"We'll take him home with us," answered Smitty. "Mistress will doctor him—if he doesn't die before we get there." Taking off his belt, he looped it around the broken wing, and strapped it to the creature's body."

"Throw him across my saddle," said Cooper. "I ain't using it anyway."

Smitty stooped to help Cooper pick him up the creature, and then said, "Lord Almighty, he's light as a child. I'll just hold him in front of me. He found his stirrup and got in the saddle. "Here, lift him up to me. Watch his wing now."

Cooper handed the creature up to Smitty, who laughed and said. "His feathers tickle!" Then Cooper picked up the lantern and started down the path again. The procession was just underway when he heard the cat again, right behind them.

"*Mao-Mao!*" It sounded indignant. "*Ma-ow!*"

"It's that damn cat again," said Smitty. "Cooper, watch yourself. I saw a wildcat in these woods once. It was big as a fox hound."

Cooper slowly raised the lantern higher and looked around. He froze as the light reflected off two glowing green eyes low to the ground. It was a cat, its long legs straddling something small and bright. Even with its fur soaked and plastered to its skin, the cat was huge. Smitty swore as the horses, catching the cat's scent, snorted and stepped sideways. Cooper, expecting the cat to attack, tried unsuccessfully to mount his dancing horse. Beeks struggled to string his bow.

"Don't shoot," ordered Smitty. "You want to get us hung?" Cooper knew he was right. Hunting was forbidden in the King's Forest, under penalty of death. Only forest apes could be killed, and that privilege was reserved for Lord Huntley, Keeper of the Forest and cousin to the king.

The cat began to back off, as though relinquishing its catch. Cooper breathed again. Beeks lowered his bow. The cat kept backing up, then turned and climbed a tree, its claws scraping off chunks of bark. It crouched down on a bare limb and watched them, switching its tail back and forth.

Cooper, curious to see what the cat had been guarding, inched his way toward the bright object, keeping a watchful eye on the cat.

"Be careful, Cooper, said Smitty. "The cats in these woods can glide, like squirrels."

Cooper reached the cat's prey, saw something wrapped in golden cloth, knelt down and gingerly unwrapped it, glancing up at the cat from time to time.

"Good God!" he said. "It's a baby—and it's deformed." He looked closer. "No. It's another one of them angel creatures—must be his child." He picked it up awkwardly, almost dropping it, and the baby started to wail. The cat hissed and stood up on the branch. Cooper looked at it anxiously, but it stayed put.

"Is the kid all right?" asked Beeks.

"I think so. I don't see any blood on him. Nothing wrong with his lungs, anyway."

"Here, I'll take him," said Beeks. "Hand the little fellow up to me. Beeks had a large family of his own and was known to have a soft spot for children.

Cooper handed the baby up, keeping a wary eye on the cat. Beeks tucked him under his poncho and smiled.

"Let's get outta here," said Smitty. "I don't trust that damn cat."

Cooper resumed walking, and the baby soon quieted, lulled to sleep by the steady rocking of the horse's movements. The three men, wide awake now, returned to their usual small talk.

"If they aren't angels, what do you suppose they are?" asked the ever-curious Beeks.

"I don't know," said Smitty. It sure ain't no bird. The only feathers he has is on his wings."

Cooper looked behind him anxiously. Did he hear something following them?

"They sure look like angels, but how could an angel get hurt? asked Beeks. "I thought they were pure spirits."

"I don't know," repeated Smitty, sneezing.

Beeks continued. "The Bible says that angels can take on human form. Remember that story about the woman who helped an angel, and then her flour bin never ran out of flour?"

"Yes," said Smitty. "She must've been blind not to notice that the man had wings, though."

"Did you see the size of the creature's wings? They must span eight feet," added Cooper.

Smitty sneezed again. "See 'em? I'm sittin' here holding 'em down, tryin' to keep his feathers out of my nose."

"If he's not an angel, and he's not a bird, then what is he?" mused Beeks.

"Maybe he's one of the fairy folk," suggested Cooper. "But my grandmother always said fairies were tiny."

There was a short pause while they all considered this. "Why do you suppose he's so light?" continued Beeks.

"Dunno," said Smitty. All the angels I've ever known were light. I don't know why the hell he's so light. You tell me why he's so light."

"Maybe their bones are hollow, like bird bones, so they can glide on the wind," suggested Beeks.

"Makes sense to me," said Cooper, "considering the size of his back and chest muscles. Let's hope he doesn't wake up before we get home. He just might take Smitty back to Heaven with him. That's the only way you'll get to Heaven, Smitty."

Beeks laughed, but Smitty didn't join in. He changed the subject. "Why do you suppose that cat didn't attack us?"

"That cat could've killed the baby with one bite," said Cooper. "I know this sounds strange, but it looked to me like the cat was guarding it."

"Like a guardian angel for an angel?" asked Beeks, making Cooper and Smitty laugh.

It began raining even harder. They rode on in silence again. "Cooper, you sure you ain't missed a marker?" Smitty asked.

"I'm sure," said Cooper, more confidently than he felt. What if he had missed a turn? They could go miles out of their way. What if that creature did wake up?

A short while later, a marker came in sight. Cooper knelt down, held the lantern up to it and breathed a sigh of relief. "Only half a mile to go, men."

Beeks and Smitty cheered. They cheered louder when they finally reached the manor gate, and their horses hooves clattered onto the cobblestones. Cooper thought he heard claws clicking on the hard surface. He glanced behind him, but didn't see anything. He'd sure be glad when this night was over.

5

THE WATCH

Smitty kept glancing behind him. "I'll sure be glad to set this creature down," he said. He rode up to the stable door and shouted, "Open up!"

A livery servant opened the door and ran out to take the horses. When he set eyes on what Smitty was carrying, he stopped short and crossed himself. Smitty dismounted, carried the injured creature inside and lowered him gently down on the straw-strewn floor. He handed the reins to the wide-eyed servant and turned to Cooper. "Hey, Cooper, go tell the Master what happened."

Cooper hesitated. "He's probably already asleep. I don't want to wake him."

"I'll go," Beeks said immediately. "I want to see the look on his face when he sees this baby." He grinned. "Besides, how often do you get a chance to wake the Master in the middle of the night?"

Beeks went over to the manor house and was escorted upstairs by a grumbling maid. Outside Lord Benefield's bedroom door, Beeks tucked the sleeping baby under his arm and grinned as he knocked on the door.

He heard feet hit the floor, followed by a shout: "What's wrong? What do you want? Do you have any idea what time it is?"

"We found an injured angel," said Beeks, smothering a laugh.

"An angel!" exclaimed Lord Benefield. "Is this some sort of a joke? Beeks, is that you? What the Devil do you mean, waking us up in the middle of the night?" He threw the door open. "This is an outrage," he began, "I'll ..."

Beeks held up the infant. Lord Benefield gasped and exclaimed, "Good God Almighty! What is that?"

"We don't know. We found two of them. This one seems to be all right, but the grown-up one is badly injured. He's in the stable."

"Mary," Lord Benefield called to his wife, "Wake up, we need your help."

Lady Benefield sat up in bed. "Someone's injured?" She got up, threw on her robe. and came to the door. "Oh!" she said, seeing the baby, "How sweet!"

"You look after the—er—baby creature." Lord Benefield told his wife, "I'm going to the stable."

Lady Benefield took the baby from Beeks and laid it on the bed. She held the lamp up to examine it more closely. She dried its fine, corn silk-colored hair with the corner of a blanket. The baby woke up and looked at her solemnly, as though it could already focus on her face.

"You have beautiful eyes," she said. The baby continued to stare at her, noisily sucking on its fist.

"Gracious, you're hungry. I hope I still have milk for you," she said.

A short time later, Lord Benefield rushed back in. "How's the baby?" he asked.

"He doesn't have any injuries. Looks like a newborn. He has the most unusual eyes. They have a white ring around the inner iris."

"Come take a look at the man – I mean the – er, creature. I had the men carry him into the kitchen where you can tend to him."

Lady Benefield re-wrapped the baby in its blanket and carried him downstairs where the other creature lay unmoving on the kitchen table, blood running out of his ears. After examining his wound, she shook her head sadly. "He has a serious head injury, Harold," she said to her husband. "I doubt he'll live."

Beeks stood beside the table getting his first good look at the creature. The kitchen maid, Rosie, glared resentfully at the dirty mess on her spotless kitchen table. Lady Benefield said, "Rosie, go boil some water for me and bring me some clean towels. Also, wake up Lizzie and ask her to bring my sewing basket. I left it in the drawing room. She'll know where to find it."

Rosie complied, taking a last look over her shoulder at the sodden mess.

Lord Benefield looked pale and wiped his brow. "I think it's time for me to go," he said, leaving the kitchen. "I'll be just outside the door if you need me."

Rosie soon returned. "I put the water on to heat. Lizzie says she'll be right down."

Beeks said, "Is there anything else I can do for you, Mi'Lady?"

"Watch him for me, will you?" she said handing the baby back to him.

"Gladly," Beeks said. He smiled, cradled the infant in his arms and rocked him.

Lizzie hurried in, sewing kit in hand. She gasped when she saw the injured creature. She set the sewing kit down gingerly, her eyes glued to the table. "What is that?"

Lady Benefield smiled at the expression on her face. "We don't know yet. The men found him in the King's forest. Would you mind helping me?"

Lizzie nodded, still not taking her eyes off the creature.

After Rosie brought in a bucket of hot water and clean towels. Lady Benefield poured the hot water into a bowl and put a length of silk thread in to soak. Dipping a clean towel in the water, she carefully washed the grass and mud off the creature's head.

"He's very tan, isn't he?" said Lizzie. She grinned. "And quite good looking."

"Very handsome," Lady Benefield agreed.

Carefully, Lady Benefield clipped the creature's flaxen hair away from the head wound and cleaned it. Threading a needle with silk thread, she sewed the skin together, pulling the edges together as close as she could. When she was done, she wrapped his head with clean bandages.

"There," she said. "Now for the wing. Let's roll him over so I can see how the uninjured wing is put together."

Carefully supporting his injured wing, Lady Benefield and Lizzie turned him over, exclaiming at his lightness. Lady Benefield flexed and extended the good wing. Then she examined the injured wing.

"It's just dislocated," she said. "I'm going to pull it into place. Hold this end tight while I pull. Ready?"

Lizzie grabbed hold and nodded. Lady Benefield gave a sharp tug and the bone snapped into place with a loud click. She wiped her brow. "Thank goodness that worked. The wing should be good as new – if he lives." She raised her voice and called, "You can come back in now, Harold, I'm done."

Her husband came back in, and they studied the unconscious creature. He had a symmetrical, oval face: wide-set eyes below a wide brow, a long, straight nose, a generous mouth and a strong chin with a cleft. Freckles were sprinkled across his nose. "His face looks very human," said Lord Benefield. "How old do you think he is?"

"I don't know," Lady Benefield replied thoughtfully. "He's small, and he has no beard, like a youth, but his face looks older than that."

They examined his clothes. He wore tight-fitting leggings and a tunic, both knit of flexible, but sturdy plant fibers. Cinched around his tunic was a thin golden cord. Tied to the rope was a small drawstring bag, filled with small, flat stones. A sling was looped around his waist cord.

"Like David," Lady Benefield said to her husband.

"David who?" he asked, puzzled.

"You know, David in the Bible," she said. "David who slew Goliath with a slingshot."

"Oh, yes. I see," said Lord Benefield. "In that case you'd better hand me that sling for safe-keeping in case he wakes up."

"He looks so gentle. Somehow, I can't imagine him being violent," she replied, but she untied the sling and bag of stones and handed them to her husband.

She turned to Beeks. "We need to get him into some dry clothes. Men's clothes are much too big. Let me borrow some clothes from one of your boys."

Beeks left on his mission. The two women unknotted and removed the cord from the creature's waist and struggled to unlace and remove his rain-soaked leggings, tunic, and undergarments. Lady Benefield handed them to Rosie. "Here, Rosie, put these by the fire to dry. Not too close. We don't want them to get scorched."

When Beeks returned with boy's clothing, they dressed him in it, and Lady Benefield covered him with her shawl.

Lord Benefield said, "You've done everything you can for him. Let's go get some sleep now. Rosie, you stay up and watch him."

Rosie gaped at him wide-eyed. "But, Master, what if he wakes up?"

Lord Benefield sighed and turned to Beeks, "Beeks, stay here with Rosie—just in case."

***

Back in New Solari, a young sylvana stood on the community platform, staring south, clutching a long, golden cloak around her slim body, her hood drawn up to keep out the rain. Her fiancé, Logos, had never been this late before. He had confided in her that a human female helped him with his mission, and sometimes he stayed to talk to her. But the sky was almost dark, and he still wasn't back. The storm had been violent. Perhaps he'd been forced to land and take cover. What if he'd been struck by lightning? She tried unsuccessfully to block out the inevitable thought. What if he was dead? "Dear Goddess," she prayed, "please bring Logos back safely."

A tall, muscular sylvan landed beside her at the railing. "Logos isn't back yet?"

"Oh, Tomos," she said, her voice shaking. "He's never been this late before. I'm afraid something's happened to him."

"Don't worry so much. Although Logos didn't pass guard school, he's better at navigation than most of the malvan-born And if he couldn't handle that little storm, surely he'd have enough common sense to hole up somewhere."

Tamara's eyes narrowed. She knew Tomos didn't like the malvan born, especially Logos and never missed an opportunity to get in a dig. "It wasn't a *little* storm—can you send someone out to search for him?"

"It's too dark. We'd never see him. If he doesn't return tonight, I'll send out search crews tomorrow. "

"Can I go with you? Please?"

"I think not. It's not a job for a sylvana."

Tamara hung her head. Big tears rolled down her cheeks. She brushed them off with the back of her hand.

Tomos sighed. "All right. If I have to send out search parties, you can go."

"Thank you," Tamara said, and resumed her watch. Darkness settled over the platform, and a few spirit lights appeared. Tomos reached forward and tucked in a curl that had escaped from Tamara's hood. She jerked away from him.

Tomos said, "I don't think Logos would attempt to fly at night. He's not qualified for night flying. Why don't you come in now? It's dark. We can't do anything until morning. Come on. I'll fly you home, like I used to."

Taking one last look into the dark, Tamara abandoned her post. Silently, they flew together to the great tree where she lived with her parents. Tomos stopped outside the hut where a spirit light burned inside a covered clay pot. Only Council members were privileged to have an outside light, and that only when absolutely necessary. Too many lights might attract unwanted attention from humans. Tomos rapped on the door. A moment later, Tamara's father slid the door panel open. He smiled broadly when he saw Tomos. Tomos bowed. "I brought your daughter home, Councilor Aarb."

"Thank you, Tomos. Her mother and I were getting worried. I was just coming to look for her."

Tamara stiffened. "I can take care of myself, Father."

"I know you can, but I don't like you out after dark."

"Father, I won't fall off the platform. I'm a grown sylvana, now—not a baby." Tamara replied.

"Good night, Councilor Aarb, good night, Tamara," Tomos said, turning to leave. "Let me know when Logos gets in."

"I will," Tamara said. "Good night, Tomos—and thank you."

Tamara stepped inside and slid the door panel shut. Her mother slipped the cloak off Tamara's shoulders and hung it carefully on a wooden peg. "I'm happy to see you out with Tomos again," she said. "He's such a fine young sylvan."

"Mother, I wasn't 'out' with Tomos." Tamara's tone was indignant. "I'm engaged to Logos. Tomos only escorted me home. It's his job." Then she said, "Oh, Mother, Logos didn't return. I'm afraid he was injured in the storm."

Her mother put her arm around her waist. "I didn't know, dear. I'm so sorry."

Tamara looked at her sharply. Her parents made no secret that they didn't approve of her engagement to Logos. True, he had passed the test and was a full citizen now, but because he was malvan-born, he would always be less than perfect in their eyes. There was no malvan blood in the Aarb pedigree. Her parents had hoped Tamara would continue the tradition and marry into an untainted line. Tamara looked, but saw nothing but sympathy in her mother's eyes.

"If he doesn't get back, I'm going to go help look for him tomorrow."

Her mother opened her mouth to protest, but Tamara stopped her. "You don't have to worry. Tomos is taking me."

Her mother relaxed. "I know you'll be safe with Tomos, and I'll pray to the Goddess that Logos is safe. Try to get some sleep, dear. I'm sure everything will be all right."

Waiting for dawn, Tamara slept little that night, what-ifs occupying her thoughts and dreams. The tree frogs started their nightly chorus, celebrating the rain. Tamara, who loved the night sounds, didn't even hear them.

.

6

WAITING

Lord Benefield crawled back into bed and pulled the covers up to his chin. Lady Benefield collapsed in the rocking chair with the infant. "Now to take care of you, little one," she said. She pulled down her linen gown, exposing her breast. "Here's some milk for you," she said, putting him to her breast. "You also need a name. I think I'll call you Gabriel—after the archangel."

Lord Benefield smiled. "That's too long a name for such a little mite."

"Then we'll call him 'Gabe' for short."

'Gabe' sucked greedily for a few moments, but then stopped, although he acted anxious as if he were still hungry. Lady Benefield switched him to her other breast, and he nursed for a short time, and again stopped. He spat up and began to scream. Lord Benefield pulled a pillow over his head. Lady Benefield got to her feet. "I'll take him to the nursery, so you can get some sleep."

"Give him to Mrs. Hogue and come back to bed," her husband said.

Upstairs, Mrs. Hogue, the governess, hearing a baby cry, got up and came into the nursery where Lady Benefield told her of the night's strange happenings.

"What a darling wee babe," Mrs. Hogue said reaching for Gabe. Lady Benefield waved her away. "I'll take care of him," she told her. "You can go back to bed."

Lady Benefield massaged Gabe's taut little belly with sweet oil. She walked him up and down the long room. Occasionally he would nurse, but then he'd spit up again. He continued to cry. Exhausted, Lady Benefield sat down and rocked him, hoping he'd relax and go to sleep. She alternately walked him and rocked him through the whole night, but he continued to cry.

At dawn, the sound of snarling animals and dogs barking awoke Lord Benefield. Finding his wife gone, he walked up to the nursery and found her still rocking a crying Gabe. Her hair had escaped her nightcap and hung disheveled down her shoulders.

"Have you been up all night?" he asked.

Lady Benefield nodded, "I'm so worried, Harold. Something's wrong with him. I still have some milk left, and he nurses, but he spits up right away, as if it doesn't suit him. Maybe human milk isn't right for him. If he doesn't keep something down, he'll die." Tears rolled down her plump cheeks.

"Now, now, my dear," her husband said. "Perhaps you don't have as much milk as you think. Our baby is already weaned, and you *are* pregnant again. I'm surprised you have any milk left. I'll send Cooper out to find a wet nurse."

"Thank you." She stood and stretched her back. She dried her eyes on her sleeve and glanced out the window where the sky was getting light. "What are you doing up so early? Did Gabe wake you?"

"No, it wasn't Gabe. I heard snarling and hissing sounds. The dogs were barking like crazy. Didn't you hear them? I'm going out to investigate. I suppose it's useless to tell you to give the baby to Mrs. Hogue and go to bed?"

Lady Benefield nodded.

He kissed her on the top of her head. "I'll go find Cooper."

Lord Benefield went downstairs to the servants' quarters and shook Cooper. "Cooper, wake up."

Cooper mumbled and pushed him way. Then his eyes focused and recognizing the Master, he bolted upright, "What is it, Mi'Lord?"

"Get up, get dressed and have a horse saddled up. Go find a wet nurse. Don't come back without one."

"A wet nurse, Mi'Lord?" Cooper asked. "I mean, yes, Mi'Lord."

Cooper dressed quickly, grabbed some cold cheese from the pantry, and gulped it down while the livery boy saddled his horse. He rode off, stopping at the closest house a quarter of a mile down the road.

An older man answered his knock. "Yes?"

Cooper removed his hat. "I'm Will Cooper of Benefield Manor. Lord Benefield sent me to find a wet nurse. You got one here?"

"No," said the man, starting to close the door. A woman's voice spoke up behind him. "Ask him in, Bert."

Bert opened the door wider, and Cooper walked in.

"What's Benefield Manor needing a wet nurse for?" the woman asked, her eyes gleaming with curiosity. "Isn't Lady Benefield's youngest near two years old now?"

"Yes, Ma'am," Cooper said, "but we've got this little angel-creature—an infant and he …"

The woman's mouth dropped open. "Did you say angel?"

"Yes, Ma'am," Cooper said. "We've got two of 'em –a grown male and a baby. The grown-up probably won't make it, but the baby's not injured. He just needs some nourishment. You know any woman who just had a baby?"

"There is Missus Jonas down the road a mile, but she's got twins, I doubt she has any milk to spare – these things have wings?"

"Yes, Ma'am, wings with real feathers. At least the adult does. Well, I best go now." Cooper put on his hat, turned and left.

As soon as she closed the door, the woman turned to her husband, "Bert, I'm going over to Benefield Manor and see what I can find out. I'll stop and tell Annie on the way home."

Cooper rode to Mrs. Jonas' house. She said she couldn't help, but questioned him extensively about the angel-creatures. He continued from house to house, embellishing on his story.

***

When Lord Benefield and Smitty went out to investigate the source of the noise, they discovered that some animal had got into the chicken coop and killed several of Lady Benefield's laying hens. Bloody feathers were everywhere, and bodies lay scattered in the straw, uneaten, as if something had killed them for sport. The rest of the flock was clucking nervously and milling about. The straw on the dirt floor was thrown about like there had been a violent struggle.

Lord Benefield slammed his fist into his hand. "Damnation! This is going to upset my wife. Grabbing up the dead hens, he tossed them out the door. "Smitty, I want that bastard killed and soon. Tell the men, two gold coins to whoever kills it."

Smitty's eyes lit up. "I'll tell 'em. Don't worry, Mi'Lord. We'll get 'im. With all this rain, we should be able to find some tracks."

The two walked outside where Smitty dropped to his knees and inspected the ground. He looked up excitedly. "Look at this, Mi'Lord."

"What?"

"There are tracks here all right—two different kinds. One I don't recognize, maybe some kind of mink or weasel, but the other is cat tracks, and they're huge. I think it's that big cat we seen in the woods last night. I bet it followed us here and tried to find hisself a meal. I don't know why it didn't eat the chickens though."

"Hmm," Lord Benefield said, stroking his beard, "If it's the cat that saved Gabe, then I can't kill it. That would upset my wife even more than losing the chickens. I've changed my mind. Don't hunt the cat. Just set a guard here tonight to watch the chickens."

***

Gabe finally fell asleep, probably from sheer exhaustion, and Lady Benefield got up and carried him to the kitchen to check on the injured adult. He was still unconscious. She put her hand on his forehead. He was warm, but not burning with fever. His huge chest was rising and falling regularly. She let out her breath in a long sigh.

Beeks was still at his post, but looked weary. "You go get some sleep," she told him. "I'll call you later if I need you. Ask Smitty to come in for a while."

Rosie sat slouched in the chair by the table, snoring. She jumped when Lady Benefield touched her on the shoulder.

"Oh, I must've drifted off." She peered at the winged creature. "Is he still alive?"

"Yes, but he's no better. I'll look after him now. You can take the day off. We can manage our own breakfast today."

"How's the baby, Mi'Lady?" Rosie asked, walking over to look at him, taking care not to touch him.

"Not good—he can't keep anything down."

Rosie clucked in sympathy. "Poor wee thing." She yawned loudly and lumbered off to the servants' quarters.

Lady Benefield sat down with Gabe on the chair that Rosie had vacated, but she had been up all night, her head nodded, and she soon drifted off to sleep herself.

She awoke when Gabe started crying again. She nursed him, but again he suckled for only a short time. He spat up, and then grew red-faced, waving his little fists and screaming. Lady Benefield walked him through the whole house. Tiring of being indoors, she carried him out in the

37

sunny courtyard. The baby opened his startling green eyes, relaxed, and struggled in her arms, as though trying to turn over. He seems to like the sun, she thought. But I can't keep him out here much longer or he'll get sunburned. As soon as she brought him back indoors, he resumed his wailing. Even worse, he developed a foul-smelling diarrhea. Lady Benefield changed his swaddling clothes, filled a rag with sugar, and gave it to him to suck. He seemed to like the sweet taste, sucked greedily and fell asleep.

Lord Benefield came in, and seeing the sleeping infant, asked, "Is Gabe better then? The children want to see him."

"He took a little sugar water," his wife told him, "I know it's not good for him, but at least it has a little nourishment. I don't think they should see the grown creature yet, but I'll take Gabe in and show him to them.

The Benefield girls, eight-year-old twins, Penny and Helen, red-headed like their father, were instantly captivated with Gabe. They fought over whose turn it was to hold him and how long they had been holding him. They even volunteered to change his swaddling clothes, but when he kept crying they began to pout.

"What's wrong with him?" Penny wailed. Lady Benefield explained that he had colic, and the girls took turns walking him.

***

Sunset found a desperate household. The injured adult was still unconscious. Gabe was getting dehydrated, and his little bottom was red and raw from diarrhea. Lady Benefield kept walking to the window, looking for Cooper to come back.

Lord Benefield said, "Watching for Cooper won't bring him any faster. I want you to lie down and rest. A pregnant lady shouldn't get over-tired."

"But Harold ..." Lady Benefield protested.

"I insist," said Lord Benefield, taking Gabe from her arms. "Mrs. Hogue can look after Gabe. I promise to call you as soon as Cooper gets back. I wish I knew what's taking him so long. Now go lie down."

Benefield's men drew straws to decide who would stay up and guard the chicken coop. Smitty lost. He sat on a stump outside the chicken coop and propped his back against the wall. However, he couldn't keep his eyes open. Soon, he was snoring away. He awoke at dawn when the dogs started barking.

"What the hell?" he exclaimed, jumping to his feet and looking around. He didn't see anything. Then he looked at the ground. Large cat prints surrounded the stump he'd been sitting on. He got down on his hands and knees and looked at them carefully, and then got up and followed them until they disappeared at the base of a large oak tree. He peered upward but couldn't see anything. He swore and threw a rock in the tree, getting showered with acorns for his trouble.

When Lord Benefield came outside to check on the chickens, Smitty pointed to the ground. "That damn cat was here again. It makes my scalp crawl to think that great beast stood there watchin' me with those evil green eyes." He stroked the stubble on his throat. "It could've torn my throat out while I slept."

"Maybe it could've, but it didn't. Why are you so afraid of cats?"

Smitty spat in the mud. "I've never liked cats much – sneaking little devils. One time when I was a lad, I was riding though the King's Forest and a big cat jumped out of a tree and glided towards me, like one of those damned flying squirrels. My horse reared and took off, and it was all I could do to hang on. Thank God, I did."

Lord Benefield chuckled. "Flying cats. What next?"

7

THE SEARCH

As Tamara lay awake, the rain gradually slowed and then stopped. When light finally crept into her room, she got up, looked out the window and was relieved to see a clear sky with few clouds and no wind—perfect flying weather. Logos hadn't come back or he would have got word to her. Quickly, she dressed in her tight-fitting flying clothes, braided her hair closely to her head and tied a scarf around her neck. Then she flew to the community platform. Tomos was there, and several other sylvans were already gathered, oiling their feathers, stretching their wings, and talking in small groups. Conversation ceased when she landed, and all eyes boldly appraised her. Ignoring them, Tamara walked up to Tomos. "Am I late?"

"No. I was just coming to get you. Are you ready to go?"

The sylvans looked at each other and frowned. A sylvana on a search party? They began to murmur among themselves.

Tomos flushed. "Tamara is flying with me," he declared in a voice that dared anybody to object. The sylvans shut up. Tomos was in charge, and no one wanted to get on his bad side.

Tomos had them count off, and the sylvans flew off in groups of two. Tamara noticed with a jolt that each team carried a rolled up stretcher—to bring back an injured sylvan—or a dead body.

"We'll stop at the malvan cave first," Tomos told Tamara. Seeing the shock on her face, he added, "Logos had been on a mission there. I need to question them. Besides, they know Logos, and they'll probably help us search for him. They have excellent night vision, which could be very helpful. If you don't want to go there, I'll understand."

Tamara raised her chin defiantly. "I'm going. But, wait, Tomos." She pursed her lips and looked down at the platform as if wrestling with a decision. Then she looked up and locked eyes with him. "There is something I need to tell you. I promised Logos I wouldn't tell anyone, but you need to know. I think he may have gone south towards a human shelter, the one he calls Huntley Manor. He— promise not to tell anyone this—he knows a human female—a woman he says they're called—who helps him find homes for human babies."

"Logos has been associating with a human?" Tomos said, his voice rising in disbelief. "That's forbidden. He'll be in big trouble if the Council finds out."

"I know. I tried to tell him that, but he just dismissed it. He said she's been very helpful, and he's careful not to be seen. You won't tell anyone, will you?"

"I'll try to keep it secret. We'd better get going now. Stay close to me. If you get tired, let me know, and I'll carry you for a while."

Tamara had never been outside the colony except to Clear Lake and the terraces on Flat-top Mountain. The trip to the malvan's cave was much longer and harder than she thought it would be. Her wing muscles screamed from the exertion. Several times, Tomos had to carry her until she could catch her breath. She thought he held her a little closer than need be.

The trees gradually thinned and patches of bare earth appeared and then hills. "We're almost there," he said at last, "You'd better fly yourself from here." And he released her to fly on her own.

From the air, all she could see was a large rounded knoll next to a pile of boulders and bushes. Tomos' crew members were standing on top of the knoll, wings spread, taking in sunlight to replenish their energy. Tomos and Tamara were the last to arrive. The other sylvans raised their eyebrows and exchanged meaningful smiles. Scowling, Tomos sent two of his guards to the sky with orders to notify him immediately if they saw any human activity. A zealous malvan hunter, lived in one of the large human shelters, just beyond the King's Forest.

Tamara looked around the knoll, perplexed. This was where the malvans lived? The place was bare—there was nothing to show that anyone lived there. Then Tomos put his thumb and forefinger in his mouth and whistled twice. Slowly, the malvans and malvanas emerged from behind the thorny bushes, seemingly out of nowhere, squinting in the bright sunlight, their hands shielding their eyes.

Tamara stepped back in horror. She had only seen malvans at funerals, and then from a distance. She was repulsed by their ugliness—their large, sloping heads, and their thick, hairy bodies—naked, even the females. Their rank smell made her want to vomit.

They crowded around Tamara, grunting, and making hand movements. Tamara shrank back against Tomos as one of the malvanas tried to touch her hair, some of which had escaped her braids and was curling around her face.

"Don't be afraid," Tomos assured her. "They won't harm you. They're not nearly as fearsome as they look. They're just curious. Most of them have never seen a sylvana before—especially a beautiful one like you." He smiled. "I don't blame them for admiring you."

"This is Logos' sylvana – his friend, Tamara," Tomos announced. The malvans inclined their heads in greeting and pulled back their thick lips showing their long, pointed incisor teeth in what was probably meant to be a smile.

"I didn't know they can understand us," Tamara said, bowing shyly.

"They understand our language pretty well, but speaking it is another matter. They can make very few sounds." They communicate mostly by gestures.

"Logos didn't come home. Did he come here yesterday?" Tomos asked the malvans.

They nodded, gesticulated excitedly and grunted in their strange language.

"He was here," Tomos translated.

"You understand them?"

"A little bit. Everyone who deals with the malvans is required to learn the basics of their language. Logos understands everything they say."

"When did Logos leave?" Tomos asked.

They pointed at a point in the sky and hugged their arms to their bodies twice. Tomos seemed puzzled. "Two what? Two babies? Which way did he go when he left?"

They pointed south and repeated the hugging gestures.

"I'm not exactly sure what they mean," Tomos said, but Logos must have gone south. That would make sense if he was going to the human shelter."

Tomos sent out search teams to the north, east and west. He and Tamara flew south toward the nearest human shelter. On the way, they saw the damage the storm had done. Tree limbs were scattered everywhere, and many trees were completely uprooted. "We can't walk through that mess," Tomos told her. "It's too dangerous."

When they arrived at the human shelter, they circled it, taking great care not to be seen as they searched the outlying fields, finding nothing. Noticing that Tamara was having trouble maintaining altitude, Tomos motioned her down to a recently mowed hayfield which was surrounded by a rock wall.

"We'll rest here," Tomos said when they landed. Tamara sat down on the rock wall, to stretch out her wings and to sun. He sat down next to her, untied a water carrier from around his waist and handed it to her. He watched her drink, breathed in the smell of the new-mown hay and listened to the drone of the crickets. He leaned over to kiss her, but she drew away from him and turned her head. He sat back again.

"What if Logos has been captured by humans?" Tamara asked, fidgeting with the water carrier. "I've heard tales of sylvans kept in cages like animals."

"We've all heard those rumors, and they aren't true."

She looked up slowly and caught his eyes. "What if he was killed in the storm?"

Tomos took a deep breath. "You mustn't think that."

"You'll keep searching, won't you?"

"We'll search until we find him. However, you know we can't see through the forest canopy. The forest floor will have to be searched by foot. It's a dangerous job better suited to walkers than to flyers. The malvans are ideally suited for that. I'll ask for their help."

"It'll be dangerous for them," she protested. "If they're caught, they'll be killed like wild animals."

"Yes," he agreed. "But they like Logos, and I think they'll want to help. They'll search only at night. That'll help protect them." He looked at the sky where the sun lay just below the treetops in the eighth arc. "It's getting late. If you're rested up enough, we need to get back to the cave and see if the other search teams found anything."

Tamara returned Tomos' water carrier and jumped into the sky. They flew back without speaking. At the cave, they learned that all the search teams had returned empty-handed. No sign of Logos. As Tomos predicted, the malvans nodded their heads eagerly when he asked if they would search the forest, and they indicated by gestures that they would begin their search that night after the sun set.

"Thank you for agreeing to help," Tamara told them, smiling.

They nodded their heads to indicate that they understood. Some of them showed their ugly fangs again.

Tamara saw the sun sinking into the Goddess' bower. "Shouldn't we be going?" she asked.

"We're staying here tonight," Tomos said.

Tamara stared at him. "Here?" she repeated dumbly.

"We need to stay until the malvans return at dawn in case they find Logos and he's been injured. It's too far to return home and come back tomorrow. I'm sorry. I should have expected this. I shouldn't have brought you."

Two malvans held apart the thorn bushes and motioned them inside. Tamara looked at Tomos, wide-eyed.

"Don't worry. Just stay close behind me. You'll be all right." He tucked his wings in tight and low, crouched down and crawled after the malvan. Tamara knelt down and followed.

They crawled through a long, dark, musty-smelling tunnel, which angled downward and grew darker and colder, lit only by small oil lamps burning in stone bowls. Tamara panicked and called out to Tomos for reassurance. "Hang on, we're almost there," he called back.

Gradually, the tunnel grew lighter and expanded so they could stand, and then they emerged into a large cavern, dimly lit by a few torches on the wall and a few scattered fires surrounded by rings of stone. Tamara shivered. Despite the fires, the cave was cold, damp and musty. She could smell smoke, and a strange, obnoxious smell which she couldn't identify, hung in the air. When her eyes adjusted to the darkness, she could see that, in the center of the cave, large stones like icicles hung from the ceiling. Where they touched the ground, they had been broken off to makes seats.

Tomos went to the center of the room and motioned for Tamara to sit down. Tomos' guards, seeing her unease, circled around her. The malvans went to their fires where their mates had prepared their evening meal. The malvanas ladled out a lumpy swill into hollowed out wooden bowls, and their mates slurped it down noisily. Tamara, realizing they were eating meat, swallowed hard and looked away in undisguised disgust. The guards wrinkled their noses in disapproval. No one spoke.

One of the malvanas approached Tamara. Tamara noticed with embarrassment that her breasts were swollen and leaking milk. She held out a bowl of greasy swill to Tamara. Horrified, Tamara shook her head.

"She's just trying to feed you," Tomos said.

One of them offered the bowl to Tomos. "No thank you, Geera," he said firmly.

Geera nodded and carried the food back to her hearth. The malvanas ate after their mates finished and left to search for Logos. Then Geera and the other malvanas bustled around unrolling bundles of animal skins, which they spread out on the ground next to the sylvans.

"This is where we're going to sleep for the night," Tomos told his guards. Tamara watched as the tired sylvans collapsed on the skins. Certainly, they didn't expect her to sleep with them. She didn't know what to do. She looked at Tomos who seemed as perplexed as she was.

But Geera wasn't finished. Next to the large bed, she carefully raked a small area clear of sticks and stones and lay down an extra thick layer of furs. When she finished, she said something to Tomos.

"She made a bed just for you," he told Tamara. "I'll sleep on this side nearest you."

"Thank you, Geera," Tamara said, bowing. Geera showed her teeth and went back to her hearth.

Tamara was sure she wouldn't be able to sleep, but she had never flown so far in one day, and she was exhausted. One by one, the torches were extinguished until only the glow of the hearth fires remained. She soon fell into a dreamless sleep on the soft furs.

Tamara awoke when the malvans came scrambling back into the cave. She sat up pushing a heavy fur off her, wondering who had covered her during the night.

One of the malvans went over to Geera and said something to her. Geera's screechy scream echoed around the walls. She sat down and rocked back and forth on her heels, beating her breast.

"What's the matter? What happened?" Tamara asked, jumping up.

Tomos went over to talk to the malvans. When he came back, his face was grim, and his eyes were troubled. "Geera's mate Geeron was killed."

"Oh, no!"

Tomos took her hand. "There is more."

"What is it? Did they find Logos?"

"They found this," he said, handing her a water carrier. "It belongs to Logos, doesn't it?"

Tamara turned it over in her hand, recognizing the woven pattern. "Yes," she said in a strangled voice. "I made it for him."

"They said there were hoof prints nearby where they found it. They tracked them back to a human shelter."

"The malvan killer's shelter?"

"No, another large shelter to the east. Apparently, he's been taken captive by humans."

"Do you think he's alive?"

Tomos swallowed. "They found traces of blood on a tree, near where the water carrier was found."

Tamara's hands flew to her mouth, and she shook her head in disbelief. "No," she groaned, and began to weep.

Tomos put his arm around her and held her until she stopped crying. She raised her head. "What happened to Geeron?"

"Apparently, the malvans stayed out a little too long after dawn, and three of them were attacked by two humans on horseback, most likely some of Huntley's men. Geera's mate was shot and killed instantly. The others fought back and killed one of the humans. The other human fled, and they were able to carry Geeron's body back here to keep it from being eaten."

Tamara walked over beside the wailing Geera. "I'm so sorry," she said. Geera grabbed Tamara and pulled her to her chest, nearly upsetting her. Startled, Tamara patted Geera's hairy shoulder until Geera released her.

Tomos gathered his crew around him and quietly gave them instructions, then walked back to where Tamara stood. "We're leaving now with the body. The humans will be swarming all over this area before long. I've sent messengers home to notify them of the death, and I asked them to set up a funeral pyre for the cremation."

"What about Geera?" Tamara asked. "Isn't she going?"

"Malvans don't usually go to funerals. They're afraid of the fallen. Do you want to go to the funeral, Geera?" Tomos asked.

Geera shook her head forcefully.

"It's perfectly safe. You'll be all right," Tamara assured her.

Geera looked back and forth between Tamara and Tomos, hesitated, and then gestured something to Tomos.

"She says she'll go." he said. "Sylvans, bring back a basket for Geera and then carry her over. "

Geera grabbed his arm and gestured furiously.

"Cancel that. She says she'll walk," Tomos said.

"How will she get to the mountain?" Tamara asked.

"Apparently the malvans know a secret route. They've never told us and we've never found it. It will take her a long time to walk there, though."

"We'll wait for you," Tamara told Geera.

The sylvans crawled back out of the cave. Standing up, Tamara gratefully inhaled the clean-smelling air and brushed the dust off her clothes. "I have to go home to change clothes," she told Tomos, motioning to her flying outfit, now filthy from crawling through the tunnel. "I can't possibly attend a funeral like this."

"I'll take you home," Tomos said. He turned to his smiling crew. "What are you waiting for? You have your orders. I'll see you at Flat-Top-Mountain."

The guards jumped into the air. Tomos helped Tamara into the air and they headed home. Despite Tamara's best intentions, eventually, her wings grew tired and Tomos had to carry her.

"Why does Lord Huntley hunt malvans?" she asked.

"I don't know. Either he hates them, or he kills them for sport—humans love to hunt. Unfortunately, humans think malvans are animals. It's not against their law to kill them for sport ... or for meat."

Tamara shuddered. "They actually eat them?"

"The malvans think so."

"That's terrible!"

"Yes, but we can't do anything about it. We try to keep the malvans hidden, but it's getting harder and harder to keep them safe. Humans keep clearing land and encroaching on them. The cave we just visited is relatively safe because it's in the King's Forest and its entrances are well hidden. There are only two other known occupied caves left, and they're too close to humans, too."

"What will happen to them?"

Tomos' forehead wrinkled, and he shook his head. "I think they'll have to move to the mountain, even though they don't like living there. The Council has given up on finding a new location for them. There are still lands far up north where there are no humans, but we'd have to move one of our colonies up there to look after them, and there are no tall trees there at all, let alone silkiron trees."

"Legend has it that the Goddess planted another grove of silkiron trees," Tamara reminded him.

Tomos scoffed. "You mean the Goddess' Grove? It's just that—a legend."

"You think so?"

"Well, I had this old teacher who claimed he'd found the grove on the far west coast of the land across the ocean, but there was something wrong with him. Every once in a while, he'd get this dazed look in his eye, fall down and prophesize the most incredible things. One time he said, 'Humans will take to the skies!' Imagine humans sprouting wings and flying! Either he was crazy, or he was getting senile in his old age. I never believed he'd found the Goddess' Grove either."

"What was his name?" Tamara asked.

"Senesses."

"I've heard of him. He was a great flier in his youth."

They flew on again in silence until Tamara said, "You can release me now. I can fly again."

Tomos released her, and they flew the rest of the distance in silence.

Tomos' advance messenger had arrived, and the whole colony was preparing to leave for the funeral. All sylvans attended a funeral for a malvan, just as they would for one of their own. After all, they had created the malvans and had an obligation to them. The elderly and infirm were ferried over in carrying baskets. Only a couple of guards and a few sylvanas stayed behind to tend to the babies.

When Tamara got home, her mother had laid out her best clothes. Tamara quickly put on her pants, dyed green by her mother, and pulled her embroidered tunic over her head. She combed her hair loose and tied it back with a silkiron cord. Lastly, she carefully folded her long cloak and placed it in a bag to take with her.

Flat-Top Mountain was a long flight away. Tomos and her father flew by themselves, and guards carried Tamara and her mother in ceremonial baskets.

The funeral pyre was completed when they arrived. It was stacked five feet high with split oak over extra-dry kindling. The sylvans lined up around the pyre, wings outspread, wing-tip to wing-tip, and sang hymns to the Goddess. The councilors and their families stood closer, upwind of the pyre. Tamara and her mother put on their golden capes and joined them. Geera arrived and Tamara motioned her to join her, scandalizing her mother. They stood silently, all eyes watching the sky for the bearers. Eventually they came in sight. They flew directly to the mound, lowered the body onto the pyre and took their places nearby.

The choir sang one last song, begging the Goddess to forgive them for their great sin, and asking her to give the deceased wings in the afterlife. When their voices died out, Councilor Evree nodded, a sylvan flew off and returned with a burning torch. Tossing it on the kindling, he flew back to safety. The pyre burst into flames, the smoke obscuring the pyre and the body.

Geera's hairy face was matted down with oily tears. Tamara put her arm around her thick waist. Geera put her huge hand on Tamara's head and pulled her to her furry side, making little strangled noises in her throat. Tamara returned her embrace. The other sylvans frowned their disapproval. Tamara thought, I don't care if they disapprove. Geera's mate died trying to help Logos.

All stood quietly until the pyre collapsed in a pile of ashes and embers. Geera ambled off in the direction she had come and one by one, the sylvans turned and left.

8

POISONED

Next morning, when the Benefields went in to check on the injured creature, he rolled his head slowly from side to side. Lady Benefield grabbed her husband's arm excitedly and said, "Look, he's coming around!"

The creature drew up his knees and moved restlessly, moving closer to the edge of the table. Lady Benefield reached out a hand to stop him. "He's going to roll off the table. We need to move him to a bed."

"Where do you want to put him?"

"Let's put him in the Green Room, next to our bedroom so we can keep an eye on him."

Lord Benefield nodded to Beeks who carefully picked up the wounded creature and carried him upstairs to the Green Room. Lady Benefield pulled down the coverlets, and Beeks laid him down on the bed. Pulling up the sheets, Lady Benefield tucked them tightly under the mattress. Finally, she threw some pillows next to the bed to cushion his fall in case he fell out.

Lizzie looked through the door, a disapproving look on her face. "Cooper's back, My Lord."

"It's about time. Did he find a wet nurse?"

Lizzie sniffed. "Yes, My Lord. She's in the foyer, but I don't think you'll find her suitable."

"Let's go see her," Lady Benefield said to her husband as she headed for the foyer. She turned to Lizzie. "Who is she?"

"Her name is Vadoma Cripps."

"I don't know any Cripps, do you?" Lady Benefield asked her husband.

"No. What sort of name is Vadoma?" he asked Lizzie.

Lizzie's chin went higher. "I'm sure I don't know, My Lord."

The Benefields stopped short as they entered the foyer and saw the wet nurse and the baby in her arms. The woman was filthy and wore tattered, patched clothes. Her greasy hair straggled down from a bright, flowered scarf tied around her head, the tasseled ends falling over her shoulder. Her infant was bundled in dirty rags.

"You can't possibly keep her," Lord Benefield whispered to his wife. "She's a gypsy." He pulled Cooper aside, "Cooper, what do you mean bringing a gypsy woman here?"

"She's the only wet nurse I could find, Mi'Lord," Cooper said, sounding defensive. "I looked everywhere, and you did tell me not to come home without one."

"So I did," Lord Benefield said, rubbing his chin. "Very well. You may go. I'll handle this."

As he opened his mouth to speak, his wife smiled and said, "Thank you for coming, Mrs. Cripps. As you can hear, our baby is very hungry. Come upstairs and see him. He's very special." She started up the stairs, Mrs. Cripps behind her. Lord Benefield sighed and followed them to the nursery.

Mrs. Cripps took one look at the strangely shaped infant, drew in her breath and backed away, making the sign against evil. "Ain't human. Ain't nursin' no animal," she said.

"He's *not* an animal," Lady Benefield insisted. "Please, we really need your help. I nursed him myself, but I must not be making enough milk. He has colic and diarrhea. He's getting weak."

"Don't matter none to me," Mrs. Cripps spat out. "I ain't stayin' here." She turned and headed for the door.

Lady Benefield shot a pleading look at her husband.

"Wait, my good woman," said Lord Benefield, blocking the door. "Whatever pay you usually get, I'll double it. And I'll give you two week's pay in advance."

The woman hesitated. "Well ...," she said, glancing sidelong at the infant.

"I'll give you a new set of clothes," added Lady Benefield. "And plenty of cotton swaddling for your baby."

"Well ... awright," the woman said. She started to unlace her chemise.

"I'll just wait outside," said Lord Benefield, backing out the door.

Mrs. Cripps exposed an ample breast and put Gabe to it. He sucked greedily for a few moments. Lady Benefield smiled. However, Gabe soon quit nursing, threw up on Mrs. Cripps and screamed even louder than before.

"I have good milk," Mrs. Cripps said, looking offended. She held the baby away from her. "Must be somethin' wrong with this child. It's obvious he ain't no ordinary baby. Is he yours?"

Lady Benefield shook her head. "We'll try again later," she said. "I'll take him now. You go with Lizzie and get cleaned up. She'll draw you a bath and give you clean clothes."

"Don't want no bath," the woman protested. "Ain't healthy."

"I insist," said Lady Benefield. Mrs. Cripps was led out of the room by Lizzie, whose look of disapproval now bordered on rebellion.

Lord Benefield came back in the room. "No luck?" he asked over Gabe's screaming.

"No. Mrs. Cripps has milk, but Gabe couldn't hold it down. We'll try again later, after Lizzie gets her cleaned up."

"I'm sorry it didn't help, but things are looking up for the adult creature. Beeks said he's starting to mumble."

"That's wonderful," Lady Benefield said, relief washing over her face. "Maybe he can tell us more about the baby."

They went to the creature's bedside and found him muttering disconnected words. They caught a couple of words, 'Tamara', and 'baby.'

Lady Benefield's face lit up in a smile. "He's definitely coming around. I'll stay with him now."

Around noon, the creature opened his eyes, although they looked unfocused, and he seemed unaware of his surroundings. Encouraged, Lady Benefield propped him up higher with pillows and spooned a small amount of warm beef broth into his mouth. She stroked his throat, and he swallowed. Encouraged, she continued. Spoonful by spoonful, she succeeded in getting a cupful of broth down his throat.

"You're going to be all right," she told him.

The creature opened his eyes and stared at her with an intense gaze. His eyes were unusual, like the infant's eyes: emerald green with an inner white ring around the iris.

"You're awake," she said, smiling.

"Where am I?" he asked, looking around the room anxiously. "Am I at Huntley Manor?"

"You're at my home, Benefield Manor. I'm Lady Benefield," she said.

He sat straight up, his whole body tense with apprehension. "The baby—where's the baby?"

"Relax, he's in the nursery. He's fine. Hungry, but fine."

He lay back against the pillows, letting out his breath.

"What's your son's name? We've been calling him Gabe."

The creature's green eyes widened briefly at the word 'son', but he replied, "He hasn't been named yet. 'Gabe' will do for now.

"And what is your name?" Lady Benefield asked.

"My name is Logos."

"What's your last name?"

"Last name?"

"I mean your family name."

"I don't have a family—what happened to me?"

"A tree fell on you. Fortunately, our men found you and brought you here." She put her hand on his forehead. "How do you feel?"

Stretching out his wings, Logos grimaced in pain before reminding himself, *A sylvan does not admit to pain.* He put on a stoic face. "I'm fine. How long have I been here?"

"Almost two days."

"Two days!" he exclaimed, sitting up again. "I must leave immediately."

"You can't," she said. "You have a serious head injury, and you've lost a lot of blood. You're not going anywhere."

Logos looked unhappy, but lay back again.

"You must be hungry," she said. "I'll get you something to eat." She got up and walked to the fireplace to get more broth.

As she drew near, Logos sniffed, wrinkled his nose in distaste and frowned, looking at her with increasing apprehension. When she dipped a spoon into the soup, and leaned forward with it, he raised his hand to stop her.

"What is that?" he asked suspiciously, like a child taking medicine.

She smiled, holding out the spoon, "Beef broth."

Logos knocked the spoon out of her hand. "Are you trying to poison me?"

Alarmed, Beeks rushed to her side. Lady Benefield waved him away and picked up the spoon. "Poison!" she exclaimed. "This is perfectly good broth. Rosie cooked it fresh today—just for you. It hasn't hurt you ..."

"Oh, Goddess!" Logos said in a tortured voice. "You mean I already ate some?"

"Yes," said Lady Benefield, perplexed. "I fed you some earlier, and ..."

"Oh, Goddess!" Logos repeated. He paled and put his head in his hands.

"What's wrong?"

Logos stiffened his back. *A sylvan does not show undue emotion.* "We sylvans are forbidden to eat any animal products. It is against The Great Command."

"Command? You mean like a commandment? As in 'Thou shalt not kill'? You're against killing animals?"

"No, just eating them. When sylvans were created, the Goddess gave us only one rule: Do not eat any living creature. We believe that all living things are related, so to eat any animal's flesh is cannibalism. Terrible things happen to us when we eat meat."

"I see," she said. "I'm sorry, Logos. I truly thought I was helping you. I wouldn't have done it if I'd known about your religious prohibition. But the broth won't poison you."

"It most certainly will," Logos said in a quiet voice. "It won't actually kill me, but my life is ruined now."

"Ruined? But, how? How can that be?" Lady Benefield stuttered out.

Logos' face became stoic again. "It's a long story. Perhaps I'll tell you sometime, but right now, I'd like to see the baby—Gabe."

"Certainly, I'll go get him. I'll be right back." She turned to leave the room

"Wait, Lady Benefield," Logos called.

"You can call me Mary if you wish."

"Thank you—Mary. I will. Can I have my own clothes back, now?"

"Certainly. I'll have Rosie bring them in."

***

Rosie brought in Logos' clothing. Seeing him awake, she dropped them inside the door and ran back out. Logos got to his feet shakily. Surprised at how light headed he was, he knelt to retrieve his clothes, sat back down on the bed and pulled them on, wincing as he stuck his sore wing through the wing hole. He took a deep breath.

When Lady Benefield walked in carrying Gabe, Logos' face twisted in concern and ran up to them. The infant was keening continuously as though in pain.

"He wasn't injured," Lady Benefield said, "but I'm worried about him. He's getting weaker and weaker. He can't keep any milk down."

"You gave him milk?" gasped Logos, his look changing to dismay. He snatched the infant from her arms.

"I gather I've done the wrong thing with your son, too?" she said, wringing her hands.

"Oh, yes!"

Tears came to her eyes. "I'm so sorry, but—all babies drink milk, don't they?"

"Yes, he could have milk from a sylvana if there weren't enough sunshine."

"What's a sylvana?"

"A sylvana is a sylvan female."

"A woman, we would say. And what did you mean about sunshine?" Lady Benefield asked.

"We sylvans get our energy from the sun, through our wings. A newborn sylvan only needs milk if it can't get enough sun. Here, let me show you how to feed him."

Logos walked to the window and threw open the heavy drapes, letting the brilliant afternoon sunshine stream in. Sitting down on the rug, he unwrapped Gabe and spread open his tiny, fuzzy wings in the sun. Gabe relaxed, and his cries gave way to contented coos.

"You see?" Logos said, looking up. "This is all a sylvan baby needs."

Lady Benefield smiled. "That's amazing. No wonder he liked it when I took him outside. It was the only time he quit crying."

"Yes. I think when the foreign milk leaves his body, he will be a happy baby again. Sylvan babies never cry unless they're sick or frightened. It might draw human attention to our colony. If you'll excuse me, I need some sun, too." Logos said, sitting down next to the baby and spreading out his good wing in the sunshine.

"Have I harmed Gabe, too?" Lady Benefield asked.

"Maybe," answered Logos. "I've never heard of a sylvan baby being given human milk. We probably won't know for sure until he grows up."

"I gave him some sugar water, too. That was all right, wasn't it?"

"Where did you get the water?" Logos asked, yawning.

"From the well. It's nice, fresh water."

"It's probably all right. I don't know. We filter our water through a cloth to make sure there are no insects or insect eggs in it—we don't want to take a chance with animal materials whatsoever."

"I collect rain water in a barrel to rinse my hair," said Lady Benefield. "If I filter it, that should be all right, shouldn't it?"

But there was no reply. Logos was sound asleep in the sunshine, his long, thin hands still cupping the child. She watched them sleep for a while. The door opened, and her husband entered. Seeing the creatures lying on the floor, he shot a questioning glance at her. She raised her finger to her lips and pushed him out of the room, closing the door behind them.

"What's going on?" he whispered.

"They're eating."

"Eating? What do you mean?"

"His name is Logos. He says he's a sylvan. Believe it or not, sylvans live on sunshine—even the babies. They don't eat any animal matter." Her face grew serious, and her eyes got moist. "Apparently, I injured him by feeding him beef broth." Her voice shook, "He said I may have injured Gabe by nursing him."

"Well, my dear, you couldn't have known," Lord Benefield said, patting her arm. "They look all right to me. At least Gabe has stopped crying."

She blew her nose and smiled. "Gabe is going to be all right. We won't be needing Mrs. Cripps now. Lizzie is outfitting her with new clothes. I'll give her the cotton swaddling, like I promised, then we'll pay her and send her back to the caravan."

"Wonderful! I'll be glad to be rid of that awful woman. Let me know when Logos wakes up again. I'm anxious to meet him."

"I will—oh, and, Harold, I don't need a guard anymore. Logos is quite harmless—a real gentleman."

"Good." Opening the door quietly, her husband motioned for Beeks to come out. "Beeks, go relieve Cooper at the gate," he said.

Lady Benefield gave her husband a bewildered glance. "What's going on at the gate?"

"Apparently, Cooper told everyone he knew about Gabe and Logos. People are showing up at our doorstep asking to see the 'Benefield Angels.' We closed the gate and keep turning them away, but the crowd is growing."

9

NEW FRIENDS

Logos awoke to the strange absence of sensation. It took a few moments for him to realize that what was missing was the noises of the colony: the gentle creaking of his hut, the low rustling of pine needles in the breeze, and the squeaks of the pikniuks. Then it hit him. He wasn't home. He was in a human's shelter—a house.

It was morning. The beam of sunshine had shifted to the other side of the room. He got up from the floor, aching in every bone of his body and moved the sleeping infant over to the pool of sunshine. The child stretched and yawned, and he stroked its smooth cheek. "Poor little baby. You and I are contaminated. What will happen to us?" he whispered.

He studied his surroundings. Although the room was huge, with a high ceiling, somehow he felt more cooped up here than he did in his small hut in New Solari. There was a fireplace, a bed, and a dresser, just like in Neela's room, but that's where the similarity ended. This room was magnificently furnished. The massive bed had tall, carved posts at each corner, with lacy fabric draped over them. On top of the bedposts were life-like carved pinecones, which reminded him of silkiron cones. Reaching up, he traced the heavily indented pattern with his fingertips.

More intricate woodwork with oak leaves and acorns ran around the ceiling, floor and doors, matching the design on the bed and dresser. On the walls hung framed images of humans who were wearing preposterous clothes with lacy collars. He wondered who they were and why they would wear such uncomfortable clothing.

Across the room in front of the fireplace were two large chairs covered with a red floral pattern. Between them was a round table on which sat a lamp with a tall, glass chimney, much more elegant than the one Neela used.

His eye was drawn to the fireplace. A picture of humans on horseback chasing a pack of dogs hung above the mantle. On top of the mantle were delicate-looking thin bowls. On either side of the hearth, sat two life-sized blue and white dogs. He'd only seen a few dogs, but none of them were blue.

Apparently, a servant had come in while he was asleep, for a fire burned in the hearth. The room was quite hot— way too hot for someone accustomed to living in the cool, breezy treetops. He raised his wings away from his body trying to cool off, but it wasn't enough. Walking to the outside door, he lifted the latch, pushed the door open and stepped out onto the balcony.

Too late, he noticed the humans standing on the other side of the gate. They pointed at him and screamed, "Look—it's the angel!"

Startled, Logos quickly retreated into his room. He pulled the door shut, his heart pounding in his chest. The humans saw me! he thought. What if they get in and capture me? I must get out of here. He sat down on the bed. No need to panic. I'm safe here, and I can still fly … but how can I go home? I've eaten meat. When the Council finds out, I'll be banished, and I'll lose Tamara. He forced down another wave of panic. I must think clearly, make plans. I've been gone three days. Tamara will be worried sick. Tomos and his guards will be out searching for me. I must go home right away. He touched his aching head, felt the bandage and pulled it off, shocked by the amount of dried blood on it. I'm still weak. Can I fly that far?

His racing thoughts circled back to his main problem. I'm contaminated. If the Council finds out, I'll be banished, and ..." He snorted. What do I mean—*if* the Council finds out? I *have* to tell the Council—or do I? What if I'm not changed? What happens if a sylvan eats only a small amount of meat broth? Is it really true that any amount of animal food is toxic?

Although he racked his brain, he couldn't remember hearing of any adult sylvan being contaminated since The Fall. And that was ages ago. There was an occasional fallen sylvan, but he always swore he hadn't eaten meat. Every sylvan swallowed an occasional insect while flying. That had never hurt anyone. Was it because insects were cold blooded? Or weren't insects animals?

What if he'd been changed? What if he couldn't pass the test again? He wouldn't be able to marry Tamara, and he'd have to live with the fallen. He groaned. He knew what Tamara's parents would say. They were opposed to her marriage with him anyway.

A knock on the door made him jump. "Come in," Logos said, standing up.

A human male somewhere between middle and old age, with long red hair and beard, both turning gray, stepped into the room and held out his hand. "Hello, I'm Harold Benefield."

Logos recognized his extended hand as a sign of greeting and took it. "My name is Logos."

"Welcome to Benefield Manor. I'm so glad to see you up and feeling better. My wife and I have been quite worried about you."

Logos tilted his wing tips forward and bowed formally. "Thank you, Lord Benefield. I am deeply indebted to you and your wife."

"Please, call me Harold. We are happy to help, and we are honored to have you here. If you need anything, please let us know." He reached into his pocket. "I believe these belong to you," he said, handing Logos his sling and bag of stones.

Logos took the items without comment and tied them around his waist cord. "Actually, Lord Harold, I must leave as soon as possible." He glanced toward the front of the house. "There is a whole crowd of humans outside."

"Don't worry. I won't let them in. You're safe with us."

"How did they find out I'm here?"

Lord Benefield chuckled. "It's impossible to keep that big a secret. I'm sorry you need to leave. We'd hoped you'd stay for a while, so we could get to know you, but we can understand if you want to go home. How can I help?"

"I don't think I can fly home right now, but I'm sure the guards are looking for me. If I can get to the roof, perhaps one of them will spot me. Then he can summon help to take me home."

"I understand. Well, that's easy enough to do. At the end of this hall is a stairwell which leads up to the roof. When you're feeling better, I'll show you the way."

Logos picked up Gabe who opened one eye and looked at him. Logos smiled at his owlish appearance. "Can you take me there now?"

Lord Benefield nodded. He opened the door where his manservant stood outside waiting. "James, please tell my wife that Logos is awake."

James stared open-mouthed at the sylvan, before regaining his professional face. "Yes, My Lord, right away."

Lord Benefield led the way slowly down the long hall. "We're next door to you, and these other rooms are guest rooms. We don't have any other guests right now, so you're welcome to explore the house as much as you like. Have you ever been in a house?" He blushed. "I mean—I assume you don't live in a house? I mean a regular house," he finished lamely.

Logos smiled. "I live in a small, wooden shelter suspended from a tree branch, but yes, I've been in a human house—but only in one room, and it was small and plain, nothing like your rooms."

Lord Benefield opened a door at the end of the corridor, revealing a narrow flight of stairs. He walked up the stairs slowly, pausing at the landing to catch his breath and then ascended to the next floor where they heard high-pitched children's voices shouting and laughing.

"This is where the nursery is, as you can hear," Lord Benefield said as they walked past it. "Having it up here helps keep the noise level down." He laughed and continued up the next set of stairs to where the steps ended at a hatch door. Pulling a large key ring off his belt, he clicked each key around the brass ring until he found the one he wanted. "Have you ever used a key?" he asked.

Logos shook his head. "What does it do?"

Lord Benefield inserted the key in the lock, showed Logos how to unlock the hatch, and shove it to one side. They stepped out onto the vast expanse of grey slate roof and were met with a rush of cool air. Lord Benefield sat down on the parapet to catch his breath.

Reveling in the bright sunshine, Logos stretched out his wings. Gabe cooed, and Logos turned him so his wings caught the sun.

"May I hold the little fellow?" Lord Benefield asked.

Logos handed Gabe to him and then looked around the roof, which was immense. Other than chimneys and towers sticking up everywhere, it was also flat. "What's that?" he asked, pointing a wing at what appeared to be a small house made of large windows.

"That's called a hothouse. It's for growing plants. The glass traps the heat from the sun so we can get a jump on the growing season. We raise and lower blinds to help control the temperature. My wife loves to garden. She starts seeds there and conducts experiments on plants. She's always trying to cultivate better-smelling roses."

"I see," said Logos. He walked over to touch the glass and wondered how strong it was. "Well, this is perfect. The guards should be able to spot me here—and it's ideal for sunning, although it is a little hot." He walked over and sat down next to Lord Benefield, forgetting the crowd at the gate. The angel-watchers, seeing him, cheered and whistled. Logos jumped up and moved to the other side of the roof.

Laughing, Lord Benefield got up, walked over and sat down next to him. "They think you're from God—that if they touch you, they'll be cured of their illnesses." He looked up in the sky. "How often do your guards fly over here? I've never seen one."

"I don't really know if they do fly this far south. I hope so—and you wouldn't see them. Ordinarily, they stay very high up, to avoid detection."

"So, you'll just have to hope one of them comes by while you're out sunning. I hope you succeed. You'll let us know before you leave, won't you?"

"Of course, I will. I wouldn't leave without saying goodbye."

Lord Benefield looked wistfully into the distant fields. "I'd forgotten how beautiful the view is from up here. See those two large buildings? That's the stables and the carriage house. Over there is the barn and the cattle corral, and on this side is the chicken coop." He stopped and cleared his throat. "That reminds me, I need to ask you something. We had an incident last night. Some sort of animal killed a bunch of Mary's chickens. Smitty—he's my man who carried you here—he found huge cat tracks. He said when they found you in the woods, a large cat was guarding Gabe."

"Gilkenney!" Logos exclaimed. "My cat. He must've followed me."

"Would he kill chickens? No, It doesn't matter. After saving Gabe, he can have all the chickens he wants. I'm just curious."

"What are chickens?"

"They're birds. We eat them and their eggs."

"I don't think he would kill chickens. He never bothers birds at home. He probably thinks they're related to us sylvans, although wings and flight is about all we have in common with birds."

Lord Benefield threw back his head and laughed. "What does he eat then?"

"Mice, snakes, rabbits—any small animal he can catch. He drops the disgusting remains at our feet and seems offended when we won't eat them."

Lord Benefield laughed again. "Just like our tabby cats."

Logos grew serious. "I hope he didn't kill your chickens. I apologize if he did. When I leave, I'll take him home with me—if he'll follow me, that is."

"My family loves cats. Mary and the girls have been trying to catch a glimpse of him."

"I doubt if they will. He usually sleeps in the trees all day and hunts at night."

Benefield stood and handed Gabe back to Logos. It's too hot out here for me. I'm going in now. You can stay and—er, eat—as long as you like. When you come down, I'll show you the rest of the house—that is if the guards haven't come for you." He removed a key from his key ring and gave it to Logos. "Please lock the door when you come in. My girls are extremely curious. We don't want them out on the roof alone. We're afraid they'll fall off."

"I understand. We have the same problem with the infants at home. We're afraid they'll fall off the platforms."

"Platforms?"

"Platforms are like your floors, except that they're made of behdar panels and hang from ropes. The ropes are made of a special material…." He stopped abruptly as though he realized he had said too much.

"That sounds like a lot of work."

Logos nodded. "It is."

"How do you manage to make ropes in the trees?"

"We don't. They're made at Flat-Top Mountain and carried to the colonies."

"Flat-Top Mountain—you don't mean where the volcano is?" Lord Benefield asked in amazement.

"Yes."

"That place is unclimbable. I never knew anyone lived up there."

"Only a few malvans and the fallen."

"Who are they?"

"That's a long story. I'll tell you later if I have time."

"How long do the ropes last?"

"Almost forever. For safety's sake, we replace the panels every three years. There are too many to do all at once. We replace a third of them every year. The old ones go back to Flat Top Mountain for use at ceremonies for a year or two, and then they're used for mulch or tinder."

"How many platforms are there?"

"Three. The highest is the guards' platform. The largest is the community or meeting platform. Then there is children's platform. It's the lowest and the only one surrounded by a safety net."

"I sure could use a safety net around my house," Benefield said chuckling.

"How many children do you have?"

"Three," said Lord Benefield proudly. Twin girls, Penny and Helen, going on nine, and a little one-year-old, girl, Louise, but my wife is expecting again. You can meet the children later if you like.

"I'm looking forward to it. I've never met human children. Don't worry. I'll remember to lock the door when I come in."

10

THE LIBRARY

Lord Benefield found Logos in the foyer, peering out through the window, the sunshine through the beveled glass making miniature rainbows on his face and wings. As he watched, the gates swung open, and the throng of people parted to admit a horse and cart. "The crowd is getting larger," Logos commented as his host walked up and stood next to him.

"You don't need to worry about them. I've posted a man to watch the gate," Lord Benefield assured him. "He won't allow anyone in without my permission. Come on. I'll give you that tour I promised. You need to be able to find your way around the house."

Logos took one last anxious glance at the crowd and then turned and followed. Benefield opened a door off the foyer, revealing an elegant room, the floor covered by a thick rug, around which sat several tall chairs and tables. "This is the drawing room where we receive our guests," Benefield explained.

Logos, whose modest living quarters at home were sun-filled and airy, found the elegant drawing room dark and confining, but he said politely, "It's beautiful."

Benefield then led Logos down a long hall where he stopped and opened another door. "This is the dining room where we take our meals," he said. Logos looked in and jumped when he saw another sylvan facing him. Immediately, he saw Lord Benefield standing next to the sylvan and realized that the sylvan was only a reflection of himself. It was like looking into a smooth lake. He went up and touched the image.

"That's a mirror," Benefield said, chuckling. "It's polished glass with a reflective background."

The room held a highly polished rectangular table surrounded by chairs. On the table sat three large, gold candlesticks with three tiers of candles. Logos knew from what Neela said that gold was very valuable and that humans killed to get it. Despite the mirror, this room was dark. It would take more than candles to light it up.

"Across the hall is the ballroom where we hold dances," Lord Benefield said. "Or we used to. It's seldom used now." Pushing open the doors, he revealed a huge room. Unlike the other room, this one was bright. One wall was lined with windows, and double doors opened to a porch. It was decorated with an intricately patterned wood floor and numerous crystal-strewn lamps along the walls. Logos marveled at the skill required to make such uniform pieces of wood and piece them together into patterns. How or where humans obtained so many identical crystals was equally curious.

Lord Benefield continued down the hall and opened two elegantly carved oak doors. "I've saved the best for last," he said, ushering Logos in. "This is my library. I don't mean to brag, but this is one of the largest private collection of books in the country."

Logos walked into the room. "I've heard of books, but I've never actually seen one."

Lord Benefield looked stunned. He picked up a book lying on his desk and handed it to Logos.

Logos ran his hand over the smooth cover. "What's this made of?"

"The cover is leather which is made of animal skin. The inside is paper."

Logos held the book up to his nose. "It has an odd smell. Where does leather come from?"

"Usually cows or sheep."

Logos frowned in distaste and opened the book. He turned the pages one by one, glancing at the even rows of strange marks and pausing to admire the decorative floral artwork. "How do you make these black marks?" he asked.

"Those are called letters. They're made with pen and ink."

"I don't know those terms, either," Logos admitted.

"Here, I'll show you," Lord Benefield said, picking up a quill pen from his desk. "This is a pen."

"But ...but that's a feather!" Logos exclaimed.

"Compliments of the Benefield geese," Lord Benefield said, chuckling. "I stripped the barbs off the shaft since they just get in the way. This liquid I'm dipping the pen into is called ink. It's made from black from the fireplace." He wrote his name on a piece of paper and rolled a blotter over the fresh ink while Logos watched in fascination.

"Can I see it?" Logos asked.

Benefield handed him the quill, and Logos examined the tip. "You cut off the tip. Why?"

"We shape the end, so it lies flat and will draw the ink across the paper." He pulled a roll of feathers out of his desk drawer. "Watch." Opening a small penknife, he stripped off the barbs and cut off the end of the quill. Next, he sliced off two diagonal pieces on either side and shaped the bottom. Finally, he made a tiny slit in the tip, held the quill up to check his work and handed it to Logos.

"That's very clever," Logos said, examining the tip and handing it back. He surveyed the bookcases. "Why do you need so many books?"

"Each one covers a different topic, and each is by a different author."

"Why do you need to know about so many things? And what is an author?"

Lord Benefield smiled. "We humans are like cats. We're curious about everything. An author is the person who wrote the book."

Logos' jaw dropped open. "You mean humans have found a way to capture someone's thoughts?"

"That's exactly right. Even after a person dies, we still have his thoughts and ideas for future generations. If your civilization doesn't write books, how do you keep a record of things, like history and philosophy?"

"History, I know, but what is philosophy?"

"Philosophy is related to religion. It's the study of beliefs—the quest for truth and meaning in life. I guess you could say apart from religion."

"Our religion is very simple," Logos said. We worship the Creator—the Goddess—and we keep her command. He scratched his chin. "I don't think we have any philosophy. If we do, it's not complicated. It's to get along with each other and to help each other." As far as history goes, our keepers pass it down from one generation to the next in song."

"You have an oral tradition then," mused Lord Benefield. "You must possess incredible memories."

"Some sylvans never forget anything—they seem to possess an unlimited capacity to memorize. Of course, our teachers recognize them at an early age and train them to be keepers. The rest of us are more limited. We need to repeat something until we remember it."

"Like us," Lord Benefield said, laughing.

Logos nodded and absently rubbed his forehead.

"Your head hurts. I should let you go rest," apologized Lord Benefield. "Are you up to dining with us tonight? We know you can't eat our food, but maybe you'll take some wine with us."

"What is wine?"

"Wine is a special drink made of grapes—we call it the nectar of the gods. Can you eat grapes?"

Logos nodded. "We eat fruit, and many plants. We grow most of them ourselves, and we make a bitter drink called so-ak from wild grapes. Is that the same?"

"Maybe. You're in for a treat," Lord Benefield said. Picking up a cut-glass decanter, he poured a small amount of reddish-purple liquid into a wine glass and handed it to Logos.

Logos set down the book and took the glass. Holding it by its fragile stem, he sniffed the wine and looked up. "This smells sort of like the so-ak I know only sweeter. What's in it?"

It's just grapes, sugar and water, but there is something extra, some sort of an activator which changes grape juice into wine and gives it a special taste."

"Changes!" Logos exclaimed, lowering his glass.

"Yes, but don't worry. Whatever the activator is, it lives naturally on grapes. If you've eaten grapes, or consumed so-ak, then you've already consumed the activator. Somehow, the activator adds something special which relaxes people and makes them feel happier. Too much wine makes us drunk. We act silly, and sometimes we pass out."

Logos smiled. "That's what too much so-ak does to us. Since wine comes from grapes, it should be all right to drink." He took a tentative sip and nodded appreciatively. "This is excellent." Tipping the glass, he finished the rest of the contents and wiped his lips. "I will come to dinner …"

An ear-piercing scream and the sound of shattering glass interrupted him. They heard footsteps running down the hall toward them and the doors slammed open. Lord Benefield and Logos turned as a wild-eyed, barefooted man burst through the door. The man was dressed in sackcloth, with ashes smeared over his face. Throwing himself at Logos' feet, he grabbed his ankles and kissed his feet. "Lord, have pity and cure my daughter," the man cried out.

"This is an outrage!" Lord Benefield thundered. He rounded the desk, seized the man and pried him off Logos. Smitty and Beeks ran in, grabbed the intruder and half-dragged, half-carried him out through the door.

"Are you all right?" Lord Benefield asked.

Too shaken to talk, Logos just nodded.

"I'll be right back. I have to find out how that person got in. Wait here."

Logos sat down, listening to the commotion as the intruder, shouting obscenities, was dragged down the hall and out the front door. James, obviously sent by Lord Benefield to keep an eye on Logos, entered the room and sat down across from him. "You can relax. The intruder is gone now," he told Logos.

Logos relaxed but his eyes kept glancing at the door.

When Lord Benefield came back, he sat down at his desk and told Logos, "That ruffian got in on a cart that came in the gate. He smuggled himself in under a load of potatoes. When the cart stopped, he jumped off and ran in the servants' entrance. Rosie was startled and dropped a tray of glasses, but she's all right. I've ordered every delivery thoroughly inspected before it enters the gates. I'm so sorry, Logos. I promise this won't happen again."

Logos stood. "There is no need to apologize. I admit I was frightened, but I'm not hurt." He laughed. "The man thinks I'm some sort of a healer."

Logos started to leave, picked up the book again and said, "I *will* dine with you tonight. May I borrow this?"

Lord Benefield picked up a large atlas from his desk. "Here, take this one too—it has maps in it."

"Maps?"

"Maps are …. physical pictures of the land. You'll understand as soon as you see them."

Logos nodded and tucked the books under his arm. "Thank you."

"Get some rest now," Benefield said. "I'll send James to fetch you when dinner is ready."

11

DINNER

That evening, Logos joined the Benefields for dinner. Knowing his aversion to meat, they served bowls of fruit and vegetables, and freshly baked rolls.

"What smells so wonderful?" Logos asked, sniffing the air appreciatively.

"Bread," Benefield said as he broke open a roll. "It's just flour and water mixed into dough and baked in a hot place called an oven. Since flour comes from wheat, which is a plant we grow ourselves, you should be able to eat it."

"That's right," Lady Benefield added. "We put butter on ours—butter is made from cow's milk, so you can't eat it—but you might try some strawberry jam on it instead. Jam is fruit cooked with sugar—also from plants."

"I'll try it," said Logos. "I love strawberries."

When a bowl of strawberry jam was brought in. Logos spread it on the bread and took a bite. "This is extremely sweet," he said, "but good. If we grew wheat, we could make bread at home. We grow strawberries on Flat-Top Mountain."

"What would you use for an oven?" Lord Benefield asked.

"We have something similar on Flat Top Mountain which we use for hardening clay. It's probably much too hot, but we could make a smaller version." Logos stared into space and mused, "Bread would add variety to our meals, and it's light enough to carry with us during flight. Of course, we'd only need it when there was no sunshine."

"I'll give you some wheat seed to take home with you," Lady Benefield said. "I'm sure you could grow wheat. It's not hard to grow."

Logos thanked her and watched as a servant poured wine from a glass container and set a full glass next to him. He took a taste.

"I like this," he said. He drank half the contents.

If you like, I can give you some cuttings from our grape vines to take home."

"That would be wonderful," Logos said. A few moments later he set down his glass and said, "My head feels funny. Am I getting drunk?"

The Benefields laughed. "Wine is meant to be sipped," Lady Benefield explained, "but one glass shouldn't make you drunk—at least it wouldn't us. Speaking of drunk … I saw your cat today—Gilkenney, don't you call him? Guess what he did?"

"What did he do now?" Logos asked anxiously. "I hope he's not causing trouble again."

Lady Benefield shook her head. "I was gathering herbs from the garden when he glided down from the apple tree and landed in the catnip patch. First, he walked around sniffing. Then he lay down rolled in it. He got up and ate it until he started swaying. I tried to catch him, but he managed to climb back up the tree and out onto a branch. I expected him to lie down and sleep it off, but he kept walking until he fell off the end of the branch. I ran over to see if he was hurt, but he just lay there with his eyes shut, purring."

Logos threw back his head and laughed an infectious laugh. Lord Benefield joined in, and Lady Benefield laughed until tears rolled down her face. She brushed them off with the back of her hands.

"Maybe the catnip will keep him away from your chickens," Logos said.

"Logos!" Lord Benefield interrupted. "With all the excitement, I forgot to tell you. James said the men found a dead mink near the coop. Gilkenney wasn't the chicken-killer at all."

"*Whew*," Logos breathed out. "I'm relieved to hear that. I didn't think he'd kill chickens, but since he's never been around them before, I wasn't sure."

"Well, he's completely innocent," Lord Benefield said.

"I have some good news, too," Lady Benefield told her husband. "James delivered a note from Huntley Manor."

At the mention of Huntley Manor, Logos glanced up with interest.

"Leutha finally had a healthy baby—a boy, and an heir for the estate. They named him Leuthur for the two of them, Leutha and Arthur."

Logos smiled. Thanks to Neela's midwifery, he thought.

Unaware of her guest's sudden interest, Lady Benefield continued, "Leutha still isn't in good health, so she hasn't set a date for the christening, but she asked if we'd be godparents. I wrote back and told her we would."

Lord Benefield frowned. "I wish you hadn't done that."

"I know you don't care for her husband," his wife said. "Neither do I, but Leutha is my cousin, and I couldn't refuse. I didn't think you'd mind. I can always make an excuse if you'd rather not go."

"No, don't worry, dear. I'll try to get along with Huntley—just for you."

Lady Benefield beamed. "Thank you. The party won't last long. We won't have to stay overnight."

"Speaking of Huntley," Lord Benefield said, "did she tell you that one of his men was killed a couple of nights ago."

"Killed?" Lady Benefield said. "What happened?"

"His men were attacked by forest apes in the King's Forest. Knowing how much Huntley wants to capture another one of the apes, I suspect it was the other way around. His men managed to kill one of the apes, but when they went back, they couldn't find a trace of the carcass. They thought maybe the wolves had dragged its body off."

Logos' eyes locked on his host. "What are forest apes?" he asked, fearing he knew the answer.

"I've never actually seen one," Lord Benefield said, "but I'm told they look almost human, except that they're covered with hair, like an ape. They have sloped foreheads, thick ridges over their eyes, big jaws and leathery hands. They look ferocious. I've never heard of them attacking humans or livestock though …"

Logos' expression had turned to dismay. "What's the matter, Logos?" Lord Benefield asked.

"It must be a malvan they killed," he answered in a choked voice.

"What's a malvan?" Lord Benefield asked.

"You mentioned them before. You said that some of them live on the mountain," Lady Benefield said.

Logos nodded. "Malvans look just like what you described, but they aren't animals." His eyes flashed with indignation. "They're intelligent, loving beings."

The Benefields both had a doubtful expression on their faces. "Intelligent?" Lord Benefield repeated. "You mean they can talk?"

"Not like we do, but they understand us, and they have their own language. They communicate with hand signals and gestures." Logos paused to think, and then said, "He must've been killed the night I had my accident or soon after. I wonder who he was? I know them all. Many of them are my friends."

"Logos, I am so sorry," Lady Benefield said.

"You said Lord Huntley is trying to capture a malvan *again*," Logos asked his host. "Do you mean he's already captured one?"

"Yes. Several years back he caught one and caged it. He charged admission and made a healthy profit. The creature didn't live long though. The dogs got to it and ripped it to pieces."

Logos shivered in revulsion and felt blood rush to his head. The thought came unbidden into his mind: I've been in Huntley's house many times. Now I wish I'd strangled him!

A sylvan does not commit acts of violence, the voice in his head admonished.

Ashamed of himself, Logos grew quiet as he took deep breaths to slow down his heartbeat. Believing he was grieving for his friend, the Benefields tactfully left him alone and discussed household matters for the rest of the meal.

***

After dinner, the Benefields invited Logos to join them in the library. He went but declined a glass of port. "I've had enough," he told them, but he knew he needed to have a clear head in case someone else broke in.

"I showed Logos through the house today," Benefield told his wife.

"Yes," Logos said. "I'm especially interested in your glass house, which would be helpful to us sylvans, too. How long can you extend the growing season?"

"I can start plants three or four weeks before the last frost."

"That's excellent. And your husband said you can change the characteristics of plants?"

"Sometimes I can," Lady Benefield answered. "It seems to depend on the variety of plant. Occasionally, when I cross plants, I can get them to breed true. Other times, I get a mixture, and the plants never breed true. Unknown factors must be at work."

"Do you try this with animals, too?"

"The animals are Harold's department. He's managed to breed a line of white sheep with extra-long wool. That's important, because long wool is easier to spin into yarn, and white wool absorbs dye easier. If we only breed sheep with the right traits, eventually they breed true. The same thing is true with other animals—dogs especially. That's how terriers and hounds came about."

"I see," Logos said. "We don't raise dogs, only cats. They keep down the mice and pikniuks that gnaw on our ropes. Have you ever bred two different animals and got a completely new animal?"

Suspecting he was joking, Lady Benefield glanced quickly at Logos, but his face was serious. "No," she said. "That's impossible. They're two different species. Dogs only give birth to dogs, and sheep to sheep. By definition, that's what a species is."

"Then where do new species come from?" Logos asked.

"There are no new species," Lady Benefield said, perplexed. "God created all species at the time of creation. No new species have been created since."

"Oh, but there have been!" Logos exclaimed.

12

THE FALL

"Why do you say a new species can be created?" Lady Benefield asked Logos, taking another sip of port.

"Because it happened to us sylvans," explained Logos. "It happened twice."

Lord Benefield settled back into the cushions of his chair. "Tell us about it."

"Well," Logos said, wondering where to start. "After the Goddess created us, sylvans lived in harmony with nature for countless years. More than we can count. We call that period of time the Peaceful Time. A great prophet had warned us that some day we would break The Great Command and incur the Goddess' wrath. We listened out of respect, but didn't believe it could happen. Then, one day, the volcano exploded, destroying the original colony of Solari. A towering cloud of dust crept over the sky, cutting off the light of the sun—and our source of nourishment. The darkness lasted for weeks. Our strongest flyers tried to fly above the dust clouds, but the air became too thin, forcing them down. For the first time in our existence, we grew really hungry. We wondered what we had done wrong to incur the Goddess' displeasure."

Logos' voice broke, and he paused to compose himself. The Benefields sat spellbound. Logos resumed his story. " 'Wait, wait,' our elders counseled. 'The dust will settle, and the sunshine will return. We must hold out until then.' "

"But, the mothers couldn't bear to hear their children crying. They begged the elders to let them eat plants. Finally, the elders agreed. We dug through the ash for food and brought back plants, which we ate with no noticeable ill effects. But the young males were not satisfied—they were always ravenously hungry, always searching for food ..."

Lady Benefield smiled knowingly. "Young people are always hungry."

"That's true," Logos agreed. "The young need much more sunshine."

Logos wondered why the Benefields smiled as though he had made a joke. He continued, "For some reason, the Earth had more electrical storms after the explosion. The lightning started raging firestorms, which blackened many trees and killed many beasts on the ground—those scrawny animals which had somehow managed to eak out an existence. A party of young males came across one of the roasted remains. 'This animal is not alive,' they reasoned. 'We did not kill it, so we are not breaking the command.' Without asking the elders for guidance, they ate the meat. When the elders found out, they were furious. They ordered the transgressors to never eat meat again. They complied, and for a while, all seemed well. Eventually, the ash settled, and the blessed sun finally appeared in the sky. Everyone thought their troubles were over."

Logos shook his head sadly. "Their troubles were just beginning. The young transgressors grew restless, quarrelsome, and began to fight. We had our first murder. The murderer was cast out, but the unrest troubled the whole tribe. They tried to soothe things over and forget. Then disaster struck. The youths married, and their wives gave birth to deformed babies."

"Deformed!" exclaimed Lady Benefield. "What do you mean?"

"They gave birth to wingless creatures—large, heavy-bodied babies covered with thick, dark hair, like animals."

"Forest apes—I mean malvans?" she asked.

"Yes. They didn't realize it right away, but the babies were a new species—even though you say that's not possible, Lady Mary. The meat must've damaged our seed …" Logos blushed to his wing tips. "Excuse me, Lady Mary. We called the new creatures 'malvans', which means 'ill-formed people'. They could not live on sunshine. Their eyes were weak, and they turned away from light. Some said they were monsters, an insult to the Goddess, and should be killed."

Lady Benefield gasped. "Surely not!"

Logos shook his head. "Of course not, we couldn't do that. The Great Command forbids killing, but the males were exiled to Flat-Top Mountain so they couldn't father any more malvans. Eventually, they became known as the fallen, or flagits, although flagit is a derogatory term I shouldn't use in front of a lady."

"Very curious," Lord Benefield said.

"No one knew what to do with them. At first, they got along on the sylvanas' milk. But sylvanas are small, and malvan babies are large. Before long, the sylvanas couldn't supply them with enough milk, so they fed them goats milk. That worked for a while, but as soon as they learned to walk, the malvan babies began to forage for themselves. They caught and ate bugs, and worms, then small animals. They craved raw meat."

Lady Benefield made a face and shuddered.

"We were horrified, too. As the malvans matured, it became clear they were intelligent, even though they weren't able to speak. They understood us and communicated with grunts and hand signals. We built them shelters out of tree limbs and they moved into them, coming out in the evening to hunt.

"Flat-Top Mountain?" Lord Benefield interrupted. "That's where you said the platforms are woven. Are the fallen the ones who weave the platforms for you?"

"No. That's done by us sylvans. There are very few fallen, and to this day they dislike physical work except for hunting and playing games."

Benefield waved his hand. "Sorry for the interruption. Please continue."

"After the malvans left, the colony thought everything was going to be all right, but when the malvans grew old enough to mate, a strange thing happened."

"What?" asked the Benefields, leaning forward in their chairs.

"Instead of giving birth to malvan babies, as you would expect, the malvans had a mixture of babies. Half were malvans, like themselves, but about a fourth were *another* new species, different from sylvans or malvans—also wingless, but hairless, extremely intelligent, vocal, curious, inventive, and aggressive ..."

"People!" exclaimed Lady Benefield.

Logos smiled. "Yes. They came to be called 'whovan', then 'human', meaning the clever ones or those who question. No one knew what to do with them either. The malvans, who love babies, wanted to keep them, but when they grew up, the humans realized they were different, and preferred the company of their own kind. Inevitably, they moved away and formed their own colonies. We held our breath when they began to mate, but to our immense relief, they bred true. The rest is history. They were extremely fertile, although short-lived, and multiplied rapidly. They overran the Earth, cut down the forests, killed all the animals, and built huge cities. They polluted the air with their fires and the water with their waste. They started wars and killed many." Logos stopped. "I beg your pardon."

"What you say is true, Logos," Benefield said.

Lady Benefield nodded in agreement. "And the malvans? They obviously still exist. How did they survive?"

"Humans destroyed their above-ground shelters years ago. With our help, they built a system of underground chambers and connecting tunnels. They're cleverly hidden. Unless you know where they are, you'd never find them."

Lady Benefield was quiet for a long time. "Logos," she said slowly. "Malvans also give birth to sylvan babies, don't they?"

Logos' eyebrows shot up. "Yes, but how did you guess?"

"It's simple math. You said half were malvan, one fourth human. You didn't say what the other fourth were, but they had to be sylvans. I figured it out from my plant studies. Often when I cross red-flowering plants with white-flowering ones, the resulting plants all have red flowers, but if I cross two red-flowering plants from this second generation, the third generation is about half red, one-fourth white and one-fourth pink, as though they somehow preserve and pass along the characteristics of the original generation. I've often wondered why that happens, but it seems to be a rule of nature, so I suspected the same thing happened with the malvans."

"You're right, but I must ask you not to tell anyone," Logos said, his eyes beseeching hers.

"Don't worry. Your secret is safe with me." She laughed. "Apes give birth to flying creatures? No one would believe me anyway." She continued, "Gabe is a malvan-born sylvan, isn't he?"

"Yes," admitted Logos, "And so am I."

"You, too? Then you have malvan relatives?" Lord Benefield asked.

"That's correct. My parents were malvans from the northernmost cave, but the cave was discovered and they died in a human raid. I was taken from them at birth and adopted out to a childless couple. When I grew up, I came to the main colony for training, got a job as mediator and stayed."

"Is that what you were doing the night you were injured—rescuing Gabe and taking him home?" Lord Benefield asked.

Logos nodded.

"That's a terrible job—taking children away from their mothers!" Lady Benefield exclaimed.

"Yes, we malvan-born sylvans get the jobs no one else wants," Logos told them. "Like all mothers, malvanas love their babies. I have to take their non-malvan infants—both human and sylvan—away from them, before they grow too attached, *and* before they feed the sylvan babies. Although the malvanas have been told over and over why they can't feed sylvan babies, not feeding them goes against their maternal instincts. I leave the human babies where they'll be found and adopted, and I take the sylvan babies home. They're cared for until adoptive parents can be found."

Logos paused. "As you can tell, I wasn't completely open with you. You assumed Gabe was my son, and I let you think so, rather than try to explain, but he's not."

They were interrupted by a knock on the door. Mrs. Hogue entered. "Excuse me, Mi'Lady," she said, "the girls are ready for bed. Can you come up and kiss them goodnight?"

"Can they come down? I'd love to meet them," Logos said to Lady Benefield.

Lady Benefield smiled. "Bring them down, Mrs. Hogue."

A short time later, two excited little girls came running into the room ahead of their governess who was carrying the baby. They saw Logos and ran up to their mother, suddenly shy.

Logos bowed. "Which one of you is Helen and which one is Penny?" he asked.

"I'm Helen, and this is Penny," said Helen, motioning to Helen. "She has more freckles than I do." She pointed to the baby. "And that's our baby sister, Louise."

Logos studied Penny's face. "Yes, she does. She has as many freckles as I do. I hear you two have been taking care of Gabe."

"Yes," Penny said. "It's ever so much fun, but Mother says he needs to be out in the sun more, so he won't cry so much."

Logos smiled. "That's right. Tomorrow morning, I'm taking Gabe out on the roof to sun. Would you like to join us?"

"Oh, yes," they squealed, and turned to their mother with pleading eyes. "May we, Mother? Please!"

Lady Benefield melted. "Well, all right—on these conditions—as long as Logos is with you—*and* if you promise to stay away from the edge of the roof."

"We promise!" they shouted in unison.

Lady Benefield kissed them. "Off to bed with you," she said, pushing them towards Mrs. Hogue.

"Goodnight, Mr. Logos, sir," they said, exiting. Their excited chatter echoed down the long hall.

"Mrs. Hogue will have a hard time to get them to sleep tonight," Lady Benefield said, laughing. "You sure you don't mind taking them for a picnic, Logos?"

"I'm looking forward to it," he said.

Lady Benefield got up to leave. "Your story was fascinating. Thank you for confiding in us."

Logos stood and bowed. "Goodnight, Lady Mary. I look forward to hearing more about your experiments."

After she left, Logos told Lord Benefield, "I returned your book of maps. It's very interesting, but it has some errors."

"Errors?" Benefield pulled the book off the shelf and handed it to Logos. "Show me. McLutheon has the most up-to-date maps in existence."

Logos had marked a page with a feather. He opened the book to a map of one of the northern islands and pointed with the feather. "This island is actually a peninsula, not an island." He touched the feather to the map. "It

89

connects to the mainland right here, and over here they left out an island completely."

"How do you know this?"

"I'm very familiar with this area," Logos said casually. "All sylvans are—at least all male sylvans."

"You are?" Lord Benefield asked in surprise.

"Yes. We're born with a good sense of direction, but all males also have several months of basic navigational training. As part of the training, we're required to memorize all physical landmarks in the area, so we can find our way home."

"Sort of like our river pilots," Lord Benefield said. "They're required to memorize all details on the river—towns, bends, sandbars and the like."

Logos nodded. "Yes, except that we identify landmarks from the sky. At the end of our training, we are blindfolded and taken to various locations out of sight of the colony and dropped off to see if we can find our way home."

"How far away have you flown?" Lord Benefield asked.

"Me personally? Not very far. Since we malvan born aren't allowed to be guards, I didn't get any additional training, but I never need to go very far. "

"What about the guards?"

"Ah, that's another story. They've been great distances away. They've been to the great ice-covered lands in the north, to the barren deserts in the south and a few have flown across the ocean to the western lands."

Lord Benefield frowned. "What western lands?"

"Actually, that's the most glaring error. The world map has completely omitted them."

"What are you talking about?"

"There is another land mass, right here," Logos said, pointing with the feather. "One as large as the land we live on. The ocean separates us from it."

"That can't be. How could there be so much land and we not be aware of it?"

"Nevertheless, it's true," Logos insisted.

"How do you know that?"

"I learned it in school. Many years ago, a sylvan was blown across the ocean by gale-force winds and returned to tell the tale. Since that time, a couple of our strongest flyers—those capable of staying aloft for days—have been there and back. Our current leader of the guards, Tomos, is probably the only sylvan strong enough to make the trip now. I think he'd like to go, but the Council put a stop to the practice when some of the explorers failed to return."

"What's this other land like?"

"They say it's vast. There are many trees, few humans, no large houses, and no big cities."

Lord Benefield stroked his beard for a while and then asked, "What does the Earth look like from the sky?"

"It's quite beautiful—the sparkling blue waters, the dark masses of the forests, and the clouds casting shadows over everything." Logos' eyes grew dreamy. "The clouds go up much higher than they look from below, and they take the most fantastic shapes. If you fly high enough, you can see the curvature of the Earth."

"That sounds lovely."

"Yes, it is," Logos said." I wish you could see it."

Lord Benefield closed his eyes. He had a slight smile on his face as if picturing the scene in his mind's eye.

"Can I ask you for a favor, Lord Harold?" Logos asked.

"Of course," said Lord Benefield, opening his eyes.

"I'd like to learn to read. Is that possible?"

"Certainly. It's not difficult at all."

"Can we start right away? I might have to leave soon."

Lord Benefield beamed. "Yes." Dipping his quill pen into the ink, he wrote on a piece of paper and showed it to Logos. "This is called an alphabet. It sounds like this: a-b-c-d ..." He recited the alphabet slowly, pointing to each letter.

"Say it once more," Logos asked. Lord Benefield repeated it again.

Logos listened intently and repeated the alphabet, leaving out only a few letters. Lord Benefield corrected him, and Logos repeated it correctly.

"That's right. You've got it already," Lord Benefield said. "These are the sounds each letter makes." He went through the alphabet once more, saying the letter and its sound. Logos repeated the sounds, getting most of them right. Lord Benefield corrected the ones he missed and explained how c and g could make two sounds, and how the vowels made several sounds. Finally, Lord Benefield showed him how to sound out simple, phonetic words. "Your name is spelled L-o-g-o-s."

"I see," said Logos. "How would I spell 'Tamara'? T-e-m-a-r-a?"

"Almost!" exclaimed Lord Benefield, "except that her name probably starts 't-a'. Who is Tamara?"

"My fiancée," Logos said, smiling.

"Well, well," Lord Benefield said. "Now I understand why you're so eager to get home."

Logos blushed, and his face grew solemn. "She'll be worried about me."

"I'm sure your fellow sylvans will spot you soon," Lord Benefield said. He reached over to his bookcase, grabbed a copy of *The Iliad*, and handed it to Logos. "Here, take this with you and try to make out some words."

Logos thanked him, tucked the book under his arm and left for his room. He had so much to worry about—his situation, Tamara, a malvan killed. The book would help him occupy his time until he was rescued—found—he corrected himself. He was in no danger as long as Lord Benefield's men kept the crowd at the gate from getting in. But what if they rushed the gate?

In his room, unable to sleep, he opened the book and studied the pages by lamplight, marveling at the illustrations of impossibly large, winged creatures. What colossal imaginations humans have, he thought.

13

VISITORS

The next day dawned warm and clear, so Logos took Gabe and went out on the roof to sun with Helen and Penny as he'd promised. The twins carried up a large wicker hamper containing an old quilt and a meal that Rosie had packed. Spreading out the quilt, they knelt down and tore into the food. Logos sat down on the parapet and spread his wings to sun, shaking his head no in amusement as the girls offered him ham and cheese sandwiches. "Gabe and I don't need anything but sunshine, which is extra nourishing today," he explained, "but I'll eat some bread and drink some water with you."

After they finished eating, they all lay down to soak in the sun. Helen and Penny stretched their arms over their heads, pretending they were wings. Gabe, lying on Logos' chest, twitched his wing-buds and cooed happily. The warmth of the sun, the gentle breeze and the sounds of the birds singing soon lulled them all to sleep.

A loud rustling noise woke them. "What's that?" Penny asked, sitting up and turning towards the sound. Fearing humans, Logos jumped up, pulled a stone out of his pouch and loaded his sling. The ivy—which grew so thickly that its leaves had crept up over the roofing slates—began to shake. Suddenly, whiskers and a wide, furry head popped up over the top of the roof. Logos lowered his sling and exclaimed, "Gilkenney!"

"Oooh, a cat!" Penny and Helen cried in unison, jumping to their feet.

The big cat scrambled onto the roof, ran over and wove around Logos' knees, purring loudly. Circling twice, he lay down and began kneading Logos' feet with his large claws.

Logos winced. "Ouch! Take it easy. Pull in the claws! Where have you been? Your fur is full of burrs. You need to be combed out."

"Can we do it?" the girls pleaded, kneeling beside Gilkenney and reaching out to pet him.

Alarmed, Logos grabbed Gilkenney by the scruff of his neck, in case he misbehaved, but Gilkenney responded with a rumbling purr and rolled over, showing the loose skin of his spotted belly.

"You can comb him," Logos told the girls. "We'll need a large-toothed comb and something sharp to cut out any burrs we can't comb out."

Helen and Penny ran back in the house and soon returned with their mother's jeweled tortoiseshell comb and her delicate sewing scissors. Logos held Gilkenney still while the girls combed him.

"He likes to be combed," said Helen. "Do you do this at home?"

"Almost every day."

"Do you have combs?" Penny quizzed.

Logos laughed. "Not like this one. Be sure you put it back where you found it. We use silkiron cones broken in half—that's a type of pinecone. They work pretty well."

When the girls had finished, and Logos had cut out the stubborn burrs. Penny asked, "Can we take Gilkenney inside and show him to Mother?"

"I guess so," Logos said, "although he might not want to go. He's never been in a house. I'd better carry him."

When Logos tried to take the cat inside, he struggled so hard to get free that Logos was forced to set him down. Without warning, Gilkenney ran to the edge of the roof and jumped off. The girls screamed and rushed after him, completely disregarding their promise to their mother. Logos grabbed their skirts to keep them from falling over the edge.

"Stop!" Logos shouted. "He'll be all right. Watch!"

In a moment, they saw Gilkenney glide across the yard and land near the herb garden. The crowd by to the gate oohed and aahed, looked up and pointed at Logos. Gilkenney sniffed around until he found his patch of catnip, and then rolled around in it.

"Gilkenney is a flying cat," said Helen, laughing.

"No," Logos replied. "Gilkenney can't fly—but he can glide, like a flying squirrel. He stretches his loose skin out to catch the wind."

"That's wonderful," Helen said wistfully. "I wish I could glide."

"Me, too," Penny agreed, spreading out her skirt wide.

A sudden downdraft of air startled them, and they turned to see a tall, muscular sylvan swoosh to a stop, causing another commotion from the crowd. The girls gaped at the stranger. The stranger stared back. Logos walked over to the newcomer and the two exchanged formal, if stilted bows. "Tomos, for once I'm glad to see you," Logos said.

Tomos kept looking back and forth between Logos and the girls. "I've had every available fire-spotter looking for you. We thought you'd been killed." He glanced at Logos' head. "You're injured. What happened?"

"I was forced down by a storm. A tree limb fell on me and knocked me out. Lord Benefield's men found me and brought me here to his house—his shelter."

"Are you all right now?"

" Yes, I just had a dislocated wing and this little head injury. I'll be all right."

Tomos glanced sideways at the girls and then whispered, "Are you a prisoner?"

Logos shook his head. "No. Actually, I'm a guest here. They've made me very welcome."

"You know the law. We're forbidden to have any contact with humans."

"I couldn't very well help it, could I?" Logos said sarcastically.

Tomos shrugged. "What about the baby? Is he all right?"

"He wasn't hurt. His name is Gabe."

"I'll take him home with me and send the guards back with a carrier for you."

Logos stiffened. "Gabe stays with me. He's my responsibility"

"All right."

"Tell Tamara I'm all right."

"I will. She's been beside herself with worry. When I sent search parties out, she insisted on coming along to look for you."

"You took Tamara with you?"

"Yes. I was afraid she'd go alone, if I didn't. She was with me the whole time…" We flew toward Huntley Manor looking for you ..." Tomos stopped, looking embarrassed.

"She told you about my contact at Huntley Manor?"

"Yes. She didn't want to break her promise to you, but she had to. Don't worry. I'm the only one who knows, and she made me promise not to tell. The malvans found your water container, so we knew you'd been captured—Logos, something terrible has happened."

"I heard," Logos said grimly. "One of the malvans was killed. Who was it?"

"Geeron."

"Not Geeron!" Logos exclaimed. "I just took Geera's twins away from her, and now she's lost her mate! It's all my fault. If I hadn't disobeyed the law, this wouldn't have happened!" To his embarrassment, he found himself fighting back tears. *A sylvan does not cry!*

Tomos' mouth dropped open and he looked away in embarrassment. "See you home soon," he said. He leaped into the air and took off, his downdraft blowing the girls' braids back.

The pilgrims at the gate saw Tomos' departure and yelled, "Look! There he goes. Do you see him?"

The girls watched until Tomos disappeared out of sight and then ran downstairs to find their parents.

When Logos came downstairs with Gabe, Lord Benefield said, "The girls told me that one of your friends found you and that he's coming back for you. I understand why you're eager to go home, but I'm sad that you're leaving us."

"Thank you. Yes, Tomos went back to get help. I've come to say goodbye."

Lord Benefield got to his feet. "Nonsense. We'll come see you off." He turned to the twins. "Girls, go fetch your mother."

14

HOME

Tomos found Tamara on the children's platform giving gliding lessons to excited children with sky pods tied to their arms. Eons before, one of the fallen had discovered that a pig's bladder inflated with sylvan breath became lighter than air and would rise into the air. Silkiron, being stronger, worked even better. The sylvanas asked for and got precious silkiron to make sky pods to help support weak flyers, both the young and the old.

Before they learned to fly, Sylvan children were in perpetual danger of falling off a platform and getting injured or killed. Both the community platform and the children's platform had a railing, and a safety net. As soon as their wings grew strong enough, the sylvanas fitted the children with landing sandals and taught them how to glide. Once they mastered gliding and landing, they could be trusted alone on the platforms. Today, the children were getting their first gliding lessons. Silkiron pods floating above their shoulders, they were flown to a higher platform and dropped down, one by one, to where Tamara, her friend Cinsha, and four other sylvanas waited to catch them. The event was an important milestone in a sylvan child's life, and proud parents stood on the platform cheering their children's efforts.

Tomos landed silently next to Tamara as she reached out, seized a gliding child and set him down on his feet. "That's good," she told the child. "A little more curve on your wings and you've got it." The child immediately turned and ran back to the end of the line to be flown up again. She turned to Tomos. "Any news?"

"I found him," Tomos said.

"Alive?"

"Yes."

"Thank the Goddess!" Tamara exclaimed. "Is he all right?"

"He seems to be. He hurt his head and wing, but they're minor injuries."

"Good job! We can stop now," Tamara shouted as Cinsha caught another child. She turned back to Tomos as the gliding ceremony ended, and parents flew down to pick up their children. "Where is he? I want to see him."

"He's not here yet. He's still with the humans."

Tamara's hands flew to her mouth. "He *was* captured then!"

"He claims he's their guest."

"A guest!" Tamara repeated, her voice registering her suspicion.

"I understand how ridiculous that sounds, but that's what he said. He can't fly yet, so I came back to get a carrying basket for him. I'm going back right away, but I wanted to tell you that he's all right."

"Thank you so much."

"The Council will be furious when it finds out he was living with humans. He'll have a lot of explaining to do when he gets back."

"I know."

Logos stepped to the edge of the platform. Tamara put out her hand to stop him. "Did you see them?"

"Who?"

"The humans."

"I saw their children."

"What are they like?"

Tomos made a face. "At first I thought they were adults. They're surprisingly large, and of course, quite deformed. They have flat chests and no wings."

"How odd." Tamara gave him a quick hug. "Thank you, Tomos."

Tomos flew to the guard station where he ordered a carrier flown over from Flat-Top Mountain. Sylvans working outside saw the guards flying with the large, deep basket and guessed its purpose. News spread fast, and there was no shortage of volunteers to go get Logos. Several guards stepped forward. Tomos chose three, and they left at once so they could be back before dark.

* * *

When Tomos and his helpers returned to Benefield Manor, Logos and Gabe were waiting on the roof, along with the Benefields and all of their servants. The guards, seeing humans, circled the shelter and landed only after Tomos ordered them down. They stood back, poised for flight, keeping a wary eye on the humans.

"Time to go," Logos told the Benefields.

Lady Benefield and the twins cried and kissed Gabe goodbye. Gabe crossed his eyes and raised his eyebrows in surprise. To Logos' dismay, he felt tears welling up in his own eyes again. *A sylvan does not cry.* He swallowed hard, struggling to keep the tears back. In a voice full of emotion, he told the Benefields, "Gabe and I owe you our lives. I can never repay you."

"We've enjoyed having you here," replied Lord Benefield. "You're welcome to come back anytime."

"We mean that!" Lady Benefield said.

Logos stepped into the carrier, holding Gabe in his arms. Tomos and the other guards seized the carrying loops and sprang aloft. The crowd at the gates saw the party ascend and erupted into a loud ovation. Logos returned Helen and Penny's tearful waves.

***

Tamara was waiting on the community platform when Logos arrived. The guards saw the party coming, and most of the colony was on hand to greet Logos when he stepped out of the carrier. Tamara walked up to him and stifled an expression of dismay at his head wound. Suddenly self-conscious, she bowed formally, took Gabe from his arms and pulled the blanket off his head. Gabe stared at her face as though trying to place her, and then pursed his mouth and started blowing little spit bubbles. Tamara rocked him in her arms as she and Logos listened impatiently to her father's lengthy welcome-home speech.

After he finished talking, Councilor Aarb pulled Logos aside. "The Council wants to talk to you as soon as possible."

"Today?" Logos asked.

"No, it can wait until tomorrow, but we want the healer to examine your injuries right away." He turned to his daughter, "Don't worry, Tamara. Appearing before the Council is just a formality."

When the crowd dispersed, Logos and Tamara glided down to Logos' hut, landing on the platform. They stepped inside, Logos shut the panel, enclosed Tamara in his wings and kissed her. She kissed him back, then took a step backward and wrinkled her nose. "You smell different," she told him.

"I do?" asked Logos, taken by surprise. "It must be the salve Lady Benefield put on my head."

"Your poor head! Will it be all right? And what about your wing? It looks swollen."

"The swelling is almost gone. I'm still sore, but I'm getting stronger."

Tamara sat down with Gabe and coaxed the fine hair on the top of his head into a single curl. "He's beautiful. Just look at those big, green eyes." Gabe cooed happily. "Yes, I'm talking about you," she said, rubbing her nose against his. She looked up at Logos, "I was so worried. I thought you'd been killed. Tomos told me that he found you living with humans. What happened? What are humans like? Tell me everything."

Sitting down and putting his arm around her, Logos explained about his accident and the rescue. He described the Benefields and their children: their clothes, their hair, and what they ate and drank. He told her about the great rambling shelter they called a house with its flat roof and clever glass house. He told her about the library and how fascinated he was with books. "I know their alphabet now, and a few words. I'm learning to learn to read and write," he said, his eyes glowing.

"You sound like you liked living there," she said, accusation in her voice.

Logos nodded. "I *did* like it there," he admitted. "I know that's strange, because their way of life is very different from ours, but they were good to me. It was like I always imagined having parents would be. But I couldn't wait to get back here to you. I missed you so much." He pulled her to him.

As they embraced, the sun emerged from behind a cloud, and a shaft of light fell through the window, highlighting Logos' face. Tamara drew back, frowning. "Your eyes!"

"What about my eyes?"

"Your eye color has changed." Her voice showed her dismay. "They're much paler now."

"I haven't had much sun." Even as he said the words, he knew that was a lame excuse.

"Logos, what happened to you?"

Logos glanced down. He'd been deluding himself. He had changed. Tamara could see it in his eyes. He had to tell her the truth.

He looked up. "Something did happen. Tomos didn't notice anything wrong, so I thought I was all right—until just now when you noticed something. Tamara, there's no way to break this news gently."

Tamara turned pale. "What is it?"

Logos looked away. Tamara shook her head, and her voice broke. "You couldn't —you didn't—eat meat?" She put her hands over her mouth.

"You know I'd never do that," he protested. "I was poisoned by meat—accidentally."

Tamara's jaw fell. "Oh, Goddess! What happened?"

"While I was unconscious, the female human—a woman—Lady Benefield, fed me soup with meat in it."

"No!" Tears rolled down Tamara's cheeks.

"She didn't know. She didn't intend to hurt me, but that doesn't matter. I've been contaminated just the same, and I guess I'm changing pretty fast—physically as well as mentally."

"Perhaps I was mistaken," Tamara said in a small voice.

"Possibly," Logos replied. "But eye color fading is the first sign and if you noticed, someone else will too. Maybe not right away, but it's bound to happen."

"It could be temporary. The color might return. The fading could be from being in a human house," Tamara suggested almost frantically.

"That's unlikely."

"What are we going to do?"

"There's nothing we can do but wait and see."

"You didn't eat very much meat, did you? Maybe that will limit the damage," she said, hope creeping into her voice. "Perhaps we can hide the change from the Council."

"I'll try, but I don't think so. This is hard to explain, but I can feel other changes. I'm more emotional. I have a different attitude about things—like Geeron being killed. Before I was poisoned, I was aware when something was unjust, and I wanted to right the wrong, but it didn't upset me. Now I'm angry. I never used to be. I want to kill the men who killed Geeron."

"Promise me you'll wait until tomorrow to tell the Council," Tamara begged. "We need some time together."

"It's my duty to notify the Council," Logos argued. It's only a question of time until they find out, and then they'll want to know why I didn't tell them right away."

"A day won't make any difference. Wait until we know for sure. Please."

"All right," Logos heard himself agree. What am I saying? he thought. We're required to notify the Council immediately. No, maybe she's right. This change in eye color could be temporary. I might be able to fool them. What do I have to lose?

"I tell you what," he said. "If the healer doesn't notice anything this afternoon, I'll wait to tell the Council."

Tamara's face brightened.

Logos glanced at the position of the sun, which was entering the sixth arc. "I'd better go see him now. Will you watch Gabe while I'm gone?"

Gabe was asleep, snoring. Tamara brushed his damp hair off his tiny forehead. "Of course, I will. I volunteered to be the first to take care of him, anyway. Do you need help getting to the healer?"

"No, I'll fly. It's not far."

***

Logos was able to fly to the healer's hut, although his wing muscles burned with pain. He ducked inside the healer's hut and stood in the shadows. The healer wasn't there, instead Logos saw his helper who had red eyes and a runny nose from a cold, apparently didn't notice or didn't care that Logos avoided eye contact. He examined Logos' wing, flexed it, and then examined the scar on his head. He grunted approval and said, "Your head wound is healing nicely, and your wing looks almost normal. Who doctored you?"

"A woman," Logos said. "A female human."

"Well, she did an excellent job. You can start flying now and build up your strength."

"I already am flying. I flew here today. My wing is stiff, though."

"It'll improve with time." The healer sneezed.

"You have a bad cold," Logos said.

The healer nodded. "Fortunately, I only have one more patient, then I can go home and go to bed. Come back if you have any problems." He went to the door and motioned in his last patient of the day.

Logos flew back home and found Tamara waiting outside his hut, Gilkenney draped across her lap. "You got your wish," he told her. "We gained some time. The healer didn't notice anything wrong with me."

"You see," Tamara said, looking a little less worried. "It *was* my imagination."

Logos nodded, but he wasn't sure at all.

15

THE COUNCIL'S DECISION

That evening after he left Tamara, Logos flew around the colony a few times to exercise his wings. Flying tired him out more than he expected, and when night fell, he crawled in bed eagerly. He was looking forward to sleeping on his own mat and to resting his head on his own pillow. As comfortable as the Benefield's bed had been, he had missed the soft brushing noises the pine needles made, the low groaning of the ropes that supported the platforms, and the slight swaying of his hut in the breeze. Despite his fatigue, he tossed and turned, unable to sleep, wondering what the Council would ask, and what he would answer. Even though Councilor Aarb had assured him that the questioning was routine, he worried that someone on the Council might see the change in his eyes.

Giving up on sleep, he arose and looked out of his window at the stars, which stood out in vivid contrast against the blackness of the heavens, giving off their unchanging light as always. What if I continue to change? he thought. Will I become violent like the fallen, even if I don't eat any more meat? What would it be like to live out my life on Flat-Top Mountain with the fallen? He shuddered. What if they force me to eat meat? They tried when I endured The Test. I'll only be able to see Tamara once a year on Blessing Day, and then at a distance.

When he did sleep, he dreamed he was sitting at the magnificent dining table at Benefield Manor, eating a leg of chicken. Grease ran down his chin, and the meat tasted delicious. He awoke in a panic. Was he starting to crave meat? Getting up, he walked outside, letting the cool breezes blow through his feathers until his heart stopped pounding and the horror of the nightmare receded.

In the morning, he glided down to the children's platform to see Tamara. She was calm, but her face was pale and her eyes were puffy like she'd been crying. She and Cinsha were teaching basic wing exercises to the toddlers. Having just witnessed the gliding ceremony, the youngest children were eager to strengthen their muscles so they, too, could someday be fitted with sky pods and learn to glide.

Gabe was lying on a blanket where Tamara could keep an eye on him. Evidently guessing that Tamara wanted to be alone with Logos, Cinsha led the children to the other end of the platform. Logos faced the sun so that the light shone on his face and looked into Tamara's eyes. "Have they changed more?"

Tamara stared at his eyes, looking into one and then the other. "They look even paler now. They have an almost bluish tinge. Maybe the angle of the sun is wrong. Maybe they'll get greener, now that you're outside more. You will try to get extra sunshine, won't you?"

"Yes, I'll go out every chance I get. I'll soak in so much sun that my skin will turn green," Logos said. He tried to smile. It wasn't just her imagination. He was changing.

Tamara laughed, and then her smile faded. "The questioning may get rough at the council today."

Logos swallowed hard. "I know."

"Father will speak up for you."

"I don't think so."

"Of course he will; you're my fiancé," she argued, putting her hands on her waist.

"That might make him recuse himself," Logos said. "He's too close to the situation."

Tamara sighed. "You're right. I didn't think about that."

Logos glanced at the sun. The Goddess had moved it to its highest point in the sky. "I have to go now. I don't dare keep the Council waiting."

"Come back as soon as it's over and tell me what happened. Father never talks about what goes on in Council."

Logos snorted. "I'm not going near your parents. I don't want them to get a close look at my eyes. I'll come over and throw a stone at your window panel. When you hear it, come over to my place."

"I'll go with you to Council."

"No, I need to do this on my own."

Tamara kissed him. "May the Goddess be with you. I'll see you tonight."

Logos watched her go, then flew up to the council platform, acutely aware that many eyes followed him. When he arrived, the councilors, dressed in their official robes, were waiting. Their faces were grim and unsmiling. Logos landed and stayed up-sun from them, deliberately keeping his eyes in shadow.

Head Councilor Evree bowed. His bow was so brief as to be barely a curt nod. "Welcome, Logos. We are happy to have you back, safe and sound." He smiled, but the smile didn't reach his eyes.

You're lying, Logos thought and wished he could say so.

"Are you feeling better?" Evree asked. "The healer says you will recover from your injuries."

Logos bowed back—a low, respectful bow. *Take even breaths*, he reminded himself. "Thank you. Yes, I'm much better. The healer told me I could resume normal flight, and I have. I'll be able to return to my job soon."

"We'll decide that," Evree said, the half-smile fading from his face. "I'll get right to the point. You've been associating with humans—you were rescued from a human shelter. Isn't this true?"

"Yes, Councilor Evree."

"What were you doing there?"

"I had an accident. I was carried there against my will—unconscious."

Evree snapped, "Why did you stay when you woke up? Why didn't you leave right away? You know the law."

"I had a head injury," Logos replied, pointing to his scar. "I lost a lot of blood and I was weak."

"Too weak to fly?" Evree said, sneering.

Logos considered this. "My wing was injured, too. I don't think I could have flown. I'm certain I couldn't have flown all the way back home."

"You could have walked."

Logos blinked in surprise. *Walk? Was he joking? We aren't built for walking. We never walk when we can fly. And he knows the woods are dangerous.* He felt the warmth rise in his face which he was beginning to recognize as a warning sign. *Evree isn't stupid. He's goading me. Time to calm down.* He forced his mind to be still before he answered. "It wouldn't have been safe to walk."

"Why not?"

"There was a crowd of humans at the gate."

"Gate?"

"The humans—the Benefields—have a wall completely surrounding their shelter and a door with metal bars that opens to let them in and out. It's for protection."

"How curious," Evree said. "Only warmongering humans would need such a thing."

"The Benefields are not warmongers," Logos protested. The warmth had now spread to his wings. He hoped they couldn't see it.

"Why was a crowd there?" Evree asked.

"They heard I was there. They think I'm an angel—a winged messenger from God, and they wanted to touch me—they thought they'd be healed." He didn't even try to hide his blush.

Evree raised his eyebrows. "So, you would have had to walk past this crowd of humans in order to leave?"

"Yes, sir."

Evree paused as though considering. "The guards brought you home. How did you notify them?"

"I went out on the roof and waited, hoping one of the fire-spotters would spot me, and they did. Tomos found me."

Although he was waiting for the next question, Evree's next words still slammed into Logos. "Did you eat with these humans?"

"Yes, Ue-Ser Evree." Logos forced himself to breathe slowly and evenly.

"What did you eat?"

"I ate only bread, fruits, vegetables and wine."

"What kind of foods are bread and wine? Please explain."

"Bread is made from wheat—a plant that humans grow. Wine is like our so-ack, a drink made from crushed grapes and sugar—all plant materials, which we are allowed to eat, as you well know. "

Evree's eyebrows rose. *Why did I say that so insolently*, Logos wondered. "Excuse me," he said.

"You didn't eat meat?" Evree asked.

Logos told himself not to look down. "No, Ue-Ser Evree," Logos said, meeting Evree's gaze. *That wasn't entirely a lie*, he thought. *Having meat spooned down my throat is not the same thing as eating it.* Was Evree staring at his eyes now? Logos dropped his eyes.

Evree took a step towards him. "Why were you so close to the human colony in the first place?"

Logos stared. *He knows perfectly well what I was doing there. He's trying to rattle me again.* "I was delivering a human infant for adoption." *Let him think I dropped it in the church. He doesn't need to know about Neela.*

"Then why did you come home with a sylvan baby? Were there two births? According to our memory, only one malvana was due to give birth."

"That is correct. She had twins."

Evree sucked in his breath. "One human and one sylvan?"

"Yes, Ue-Ser Evree."

"Is that possible?"

"Evidently," Logos said and then wanted to kick himself.

Evree looked at him sharply. "And the sylvan baby is all right? The malvana didn't try to breast-feed it?"

"Yes—I mean—no. I was there for the birth." Sweating under Evree's relentless gaze, Logos found himself wondering if the councilor could read minds. "The malvana didn't nurse him. He's all right." Evree didn't ask, so there was no need to tell him that a human breast-fed Gabe. *Is omitting information lying?*

Evree walked back and conferred with the other Council members for nearly a full arc, leaving Logos to stand. His injured wing began to ache. He watched as the Goddess pulled the sun to it's highest point and pushed it into the fifth arc. When Evree returned, he said, "Some of us are satisfied with your story, but some are not. Councilor Aarb has recused himself, so we are equally divided. You are on probation until this matter is settled. In the meantime, we have assigned someone else to be mediator.

"Who?" Logos blurted out.

"Manil," Evree said, his eyes saying the decision was none of Logos' business.

"Manil doesn't know the malvans' language well enough," Logos protested.

"You will take the infant to see the healer tomorrow. As soon as he reports to us, we will send for you. In the meantime, you will not be allowed to be alone with your promised bride or any other sylvana. A guard will remain with you at all times. You are to go nowhere unaccompanied. Do you understand?"

Logos nodded.

Evree put his thumb and forefinger in his mouth and blew a low, clear whistle in the direction of the guards' platform. A few moments later, Tomos flew to the Council platform. Evree told him, "Assign a guard to watch Logos. He is to remain with him at all times."

A look of triumph flashed over Tomos' face. He bowed and left. When the guard arrived, Evree told Logos, "You may go now."

They aren't satisfied. They're suspicious, Logos thought. That's why Evree was staring at my eyes. Logos made a stiff bow and left with the guard.

"I need to fly. I'm supposed to exercise my wings," Logos told the guard. *And I need to think*, he thought.

"Good. I'll go with you," the guard replied. Logos flew around the colony until his wings grew tired. He forced himself to fly an extra lap even after he was exhausted.

That evening, while the guard sat outside his hut, Logos slipped out of his window, flew to Councilor Aarb's shelter and threw a stone against Tamara's window panel. She came to the window. "Logos what happened at Council?" she whispered. "Father said you're under arrest, and I can't see you again."

"I am. I slipped away from the guard, so I can't stay long. The Council wasn't satisfied. They debated forever, and the vote ended up in a tie."

"What went wrong? Why weren't they satisfied?"

"I don't know. I got annoyed with them and said some things I shouldn't have. I don't think Evree could see the changes in my eyes. The sun was behind me."

"Father and Mother said we have to postpone our marriage until this is settled. I argued with them, but they refused to listen. I've never seen them so irrational."

"Don't blame them. They're just worried about you," Logos said, "and rightfully so."

Tamara looked into his eyes and gave a little cry of surprised.

"What's the matter?" he asked.

"Your eye rings are narrower."

Logos heart skipped a beat.

"It's getting dark. The light is poor. Maybe it's my imagination," Tamara said.

"Maybe … there is something else I have to tell you. The Council wants Gabe to see the healer."

"Gabe? Why?"

"In case he was contaminated—which he was. I didn't tell them but he was breast-fed human milk."

Tamara's eyes went wide. "Not Gabe, too! Why didn't you tell me this yesterday?"

"I didn't want to upset you. Look, I think Gabe's all right. A sylvan has never been nursed by humans before. We don't know if human milk will have any effect on him. His eyes are as green as yours, and his rings are huge. He'll be a great navigator some day." A noise made him turn. "I have to go now."

Tamara kissed him. "Go with the Goddess," she said. "Don't get caught flying home!"

***

The next day, Logos picked up Gabe and flew to the healer's hut. This time the healer was there. After examining Logos' head and wing, the healer held a large, round crystal up to Logos' eye. He whistled and lowered the crystal. "Why didn't you tell my helper about this?" His voice sounded distressed.

Logos sighed. "I wasn't sure I was changed, and I wanted to buy a little more time with my intended."

"Did you eat meat?" the healer asked.

"Yes—but not on purpose!"

"Unfortunately, that doesn't matter, does it? You're still corrupted."

"Is there really no way to reverse the damage?" Logos asked.

The healer shook his head. "I'm sorry. I wish to the Goddess there were, although if you don't eat any more meat, the damage will be limited." He glanced at Gabe. "The Council wants me to examine the infant. Was he contaminated, too?"

Logos hesitated. "He might be," he admitted. "He was nursed on human milk but he refused it. I don't know if that would change him or not—do you? Unlike me, his eye color hasn't changed, and his rings are as wide as ever. I'm hoping he'll be all right."

"Malvana milk corrupts malvan-born sylvans," the healer said. "Why should human milk be any different? Hold him up to the light, so I can examine his eyes."

Logos held Gabe in the sun while the healer examined Gabe's eyes. Logos had to smile. Magnified through the crystal, Gabe's clear, green eyes looked positively owlish.

"How are they?" Logos asked as soon as the healer laid down the crystal.

"You're right," the healer said. "There is nothing wrong with *his* eyes, but I have no choice except to tell the Council that you've both been contaminated. I have to warn you that due to the circumstances, they may want to quarantine both of you."

"Both?" Logos was shocked. He knew they'd quarantine him, but he never dreamed the Council might quarantine Gabe. The thought made him furious. An innocent child shouldn't have to live on Flat-Top Mountain. He remembered the bullying he had encountered when he endured The Trial there as a youth. How could any child grow up normal in that environment? What if the fallen gave Gabe meat? The thought made him sick to his stomach.

***

115

Logos flew Gabe to the children's platform. He prayed that Tamara's father wouldn't see him. Tamara ran up to him. Seeing her, Gabe bounced and made happy cooing sounds. He reached out his arms for her and she took him. "What did the healer say?" she asked.

"He saw the changes in my eyes."

"What about Gabe?"

"There is nothing wrong with Gabe, thank the Goddess, but he has to tell the Council that we were both contaminated." Logos paused, "He thinks the Council might quarantine Gabe."

Tamara drew Gabe closer to her. "They can't do that!" she exclaimed. She glanced around, lowered her voice and whispered, "You must take him and flee—now, while you still have a chance to get away."

"Where would I go?" Logos asked. "You know the guards see everything that goes on. There is no place I wouldn't be captured and brought back."

"I can't believe I'm saying this, but you could go back to the humans."

"Yes, but just think. I could never go outside. The guards would grab me and haul be back. At least on Flat Top Mountain I can be outside in the sun, and I'll get to see you once in a while, even if it is from a distance." Logos took her hands. "I'm so sorry this happened. I wanted to marry you and be with you forever." He stopped, searching for the right words. "Our marriage is impossible now. I release you from your promise."

"I don't want to be released," she whimpered. "I can't live without you."

Logos pulled her head to his shoulder. "Don't talk like that. I want you to find someone else and be happy."

"It's not fair. It wasn't your fault. You're a good person," she choked out.

"No, it's not fair, but it happened. We can't change it."

Tamara began to sob. Logos held her tight until she stopped shaking, then kissed her. "I've got to go now."

That afternoon, the Council sent a guard to fetch Logos. When he arrived, all of the councilors wore grim faces. Evree arose to speak. "The healer has notified us that you are contaminated." He didn't sound surprised. "You ate meat?"

"No, of course not. It was accidental. I was given broth with animal meat in it while I wasn't fully conscious."

"Why didn't you tell us this yesterday?"

"It was such a small amount, I thought maybe it wouldn't affect me—and I wanted more time with my intended." Logos glanced at Tamara's father whose face was stony.

"I am truly sorry for you," Evree said, "I believe you when you say this wasn't a deliberate act on your part, but you know the law. You cannot stay here. Nor can you ever marry."

Logos lowered his head. "I know. I've already broke off my engagement."

Tamara's father looked down at his hands. Evree conferred with the rest of the Council. Councilor Aarb did not take part in the discussion this time, and the debate did not last long. Councilor Evree stood up. "Logos, we have reached a unanimous decision. You are hereby banished. You will be taken to Flat-Top Mountain and be de-winged."

Logos bowed and then asked, "What about Gabe?"

"The healer told us that the infant was contaminated by human milk. Is that true?"

"Yes."

"Why did you keep this from us?"

"Because I honestly don't think the milk hurt him. And it's true. His eyes are fine. Even the healer thought so. He told you so, didn't he?"

"He did," Evree admitted. "But Gabe is young. He still might change."

"Then for Goddess' sake let him stay here until he does, or until he's old enough to take the Trial!" Logos pleaded.

Evree didn't reply. He walked back to the Council, and they began to debate. Logos couldn't hear what they were saying, but he watched their faces. This time, Councilor Aarb took part. Logos saw him shake his head animatedly several times. The meeting seemed interminable. Logos shifted from foot to foot. His injured wing began to ache and his head throbbed. *What was taking so long?*

The sun passed the seventh arc and long shadows fell on the platform. Finally, the Council fell silent, and Evree stood and called him over. "Logos, we have reached a decision, although as you probably realize, it wasn't unanimous. Due to his known contamination, we cannot allow the child to remain here. He is to be quarantined on Flat-Top Mountain until adulthood, when he will be allowed to take The Test."

"That's no place for an infant," Logos cried out. "Who will take care of him? There aren't any sylvanas there."

"Remember where you are and control yourself," Evree thundered. He added more quietly, "You will take care of him yourself."

"No child should have to grow up there," Logos shouted, his fists balling up. "You don't know what it's like to live there. I do!"

Councilor Evree's eyes narrowed, and his voice was icy. "Our decision is final. Due to the late time of day, you and the infant will be taken to Flat-Top Mountain tomorrow morning. You are dismissed."

Wheeling around, Evree snapped, "Guards, take Logos back to his quarters."

16

LOGOS' DECISION

Logos flew to the children's platform accompanied by Poro, the guard assigned to him, but Tamara had already left for the day. Disappointed, and knowing he wouldn't be welcome at Tamara's parents' shelter, he returned home; Poro took his position outside the door. When Logos walked into his hut, he found Tamara waiting inside with Gabe. She raised her finger to her lips. "I came in the window. What did Council say?" she asked in a low voice.

"I'm to be banished as we expected, but Gabe is to be quarantined as well."

"No!" Tamara cried out. Logos shushed her. She grimaced and lowered her voice again. "He hasn't changed! He should be allowed to live here until his adolescence."

"I told them that, but Evree said the rule is clear. Gabe was definitely contaminated, so he can't stay here."

Tamara grimaced. "How can he grow up normal on Flat-Top Mountain?"

"That's what I told the councilors, but they wouldn't listen."

"When are they taking you there?"

"Tomorrow morning."

Tamara pulled him close and practically hissed into his ear, "You must escape tonight with Gabe. It's his only chance."

"Are you crazy? How could I possibly escape? I'd never get past the night guard."

"You might if Tomos helped you."

Logos shook his head. "Why should Tomos risk his career to help me? He hates me."

"Maybe he'll do it for me. It's worth a try. Right?"

***

Sneaking out through Logos' window again, Tamara took the long way around the tree, so Poro wouldn't see her leave, and then flew over to the guards' platform. Recognizing her, the guard snapped to attention and bowed.

"Where is Tomos?" she asked.

"He's over at Flat-Top Mountain."

"When do you expect him back?"

"I don't know, Ue-Mem Tamara."

"When he gets back, tell him I'm looking for him. Ask him to come to the children's platform as soon as he can."

The guard nodded. "I'll tell him."

Tamara flew to the children's platform which was empty. She paced back and forth, watching the shadows grow longer, until Tomos landed on the platform. She rushed up to him.

"What's the matter?" he asked.

"Logos has been exiled—he and Gabe, both."

"A baby exiled?" Tomos said, sounding disbelieving. "That's unheard of!"

Tamara wrung her hands. "You must help them."

"*Me?*" Tomos exclaimed in honest amazement. "I can't disobey the Council—besides, be realistic. Where could I hide them? No matter where he went, he'd be caught."

"The humans who rescued him will take him in."

Tomos snorted. "Humans! What kind of low life would that be?"

"He liked living with the humans," Tamara insisted. "And anything is better than living on Flat-Top Mountain. Won't you help him?"

"Absolutely not. I'm sworn to uphold the law."

"Please, Tomos," begged Tamara. "I'm asking you as a favor. Do it for me, and if you can't do it for me, do it for Gabe. He's completely innocent."

"I'm truly sorry, but I just can't," Tomos replied.

Tamara gave him a scathing glance, spun around on her heels and flew away.

***

As soon as Tamara was out of sight, Tomos flew to Logos' quarters, avoiding Poro, and rapped lightly on his window panel. Logos came to the window, "What are you doing here?" he asked.

Tomos crawled over the window sill. "Shh! Tamara asked me to help you and Gabe escape. I told her no, because I don't want her involved with something illegal— but I can't say no to her. And I think Gabe shouldn't be exiled. Of course, I'll help you."

Logos stared at him, trying to make sense of this sudden change of events. "You lied to Tamara?"

"I hate myself for doing it, but I had to. There is no way she could stand up to questioning. Her face is too expressive. She would give us away.

"Your career could be ruined."

"I think I can pull it off, and I'm willing to take the chance."

"I have to admit that I welcome your help," Logos said. "But how will I get past the night guard?"

"Let me take care of that. I set the schedules, so I'll assign an inexperienced guard, and then I'll help you get past him. Fortunately, the moon is in the Goddess' bower tonight, so the darkness will hide you. Noise can't be covered, though. You must fly in quiet mode until you get out of earshot. I assume you know the way to Benefield Manor?"

"I think so—at least I could find it in daytime." Logos closed his eyes, picturing the route in his head. "It's almost due south, several miles south of Winding Creek. The Manor house has lanterns over the front door and outside the gate, and there are no big trees nearby. Also, if I manage to fly directly above the house, I'll feel the warm air currents rising from the roof."

Tomos nodded in satisfaction. "Do you think you can fly that far?"

Logos worked his shoulders. "I'm not sure. My wing is still a little stiff, and I haven't flown any distance for several weeks, but I'll try. If I have to, I can take cover for the night and continue at daybreak."

"That would be extremely dangerous."

Logos gave a wry chuckle. "Yes. A tree might fall on me."

Tomos' lips almost cracked a smile. "All right then. I'll come for you when the night is completely dark. Be ready to go."

Tomos slipped out the window and flew silently away. Shortly after, Tamara landed on Logos' platform, opened his window panel and crawled in, not bothering to knock. "I can only stay a moment," she explained. "Father found out I met you on the platform and he's furious with me. He told me that I couldn't leave the shelter until you're gone, but I sneaked out. I had to say goodbye." She paused. "I asked Tomos to help you, and he refused flat out." Her voice was bitter. "I thought he loved me. What are we going to do?"

"I've decided to try to get away on my own." He put his arm around her. "Tamara, I'm so sorry this happened. I love you so much."

Tamara began to cry. Logos raised her chin and brushed away her tears with his thumbs. "Please don't make this any harder than it already is. I don't want to leave you, but I don't have any choice. I'll always love you, but our marriage is impossible now."

Tamara looked down.

"Don't mourn me, and don't be alone all your life. I want you to marry and have children—be happy "

Her head snapped up. "I'll never marry. I'll become a healer and dedicate my life to helping people."

"I want you to be happy," Logos repeated. "You should think about Tomos. He loves you, and he would be a good husband. He's a fine sylvan; he'll probably be on the Council some day. Promise me you'll consider him."

Tamara said nothing.

"Go home now, sweetheart," Logos said, picking her up and lifting her out the window. "I'll come for Gabe when it's dark. Listen for me."

Tamara turned and flew home. Her mother caught her sneaking in the window and folded her daughter in her wings.

***

Eckles was scheduled to fly the night patrol. Tomos told Eckles, "I'm changing the schedule. You're off tonight, because I want you to escort Logos and Gabe to Flat-Top Mountain in the morning."

A look of surprise flashed over Eckles face, followed by pleasure.

"You understand why I don't want to take them myself, don't you?" Tomos asked.

"Sure," Eckles said. "Tamara used to be your girlfriend, but why choose me?"

"You're my best flier. You don't mind doing it, do you?"

"Of course not. You know I never liked that malvan-born trash. I'm not surprised he got in trouble."

Tomos replaced Eckles with Stebil, a recent trainee who needed experience in night patrol. Then he went home and waited for night to fall. When he was satisfied that the sky was as dark as it would get, he flew to Logos' hut. Poro lay sprawled in front of the hut asleep. Tomos scowled, stepped over him and walked in the door unchallenged.

"Logos?" Tomos called in a low voice.

"I'm ready."

"Stebin's on duty," Tomos said. "He's a new recruit and inexperienced. I'll stay well behind him and mimic his wing movements, so he won't hear me. As soon as he turns west, I'll fall back and signal you to leave."

"How?"

Tomos whistled a low cry, like a nightingale startled in its sleep. "When you hear that, fly straight south in quiet flight as low as you safely can. If Stebil hears you, he'll investigate. As soon as you're out of earshot, fly as fast as you can. If you're caught, you're on your own. I won't be able to help you."

"I understand."

"All right then, go get Gabe. I'll wait for you at the children's platform."

Logos glided to Councilor Aarb's platform, landing in complete silence outside Tamara's window. She handed a sleeping Gabe over to him without saying a word.

Logos leaned over and kissed her. "Good-bye, my beloved," he whispered, his heart aching. "May the Goddess always smile on you."

She drew his head close to hers for a moment. "Safe flying," she whispered back, and slid the panel shut.

Logos flew to the children's platform with Gabe. Tomos said, "Wait for my signal to leave."

"Thanks for helping us," Logos replied.

Tomos didn't reply. He took to the air to locate the night guard. Back on the platform, Logos waited, his ears straining for Tomos' whistle. Just when he thought he'd missed it, the plaintive call of a nightingale drifted through the trees. Flying up through the void, Logos flew south as quietly as he could, turning the front edges of his primary feathers forward to minimize noise. Quiet flight took more energy, and his wing muscles began to burn with the exertion. He forced himself to push through the pain by concentrating on his wing strokes: up—in, down—out. *A sylvan does not admit to pain.*

Without being able to see landmarks, he was uncertain how far he had flown. He feared he might overshoot Benefield Manor and miss it completely. He glanced down and thought he saw specks of starlight glinting off water. Winding Creek was only about halfway to Benefield Manor. He hadn't flown nearly as far as he'd hoped, but he thought he was far enough away not to be heard, so he resumed normal flight and gained altitude, searching for an updraft but found none. He checked his bearing according to the stars and made a slight correction. Over the next few miles, he continued to battle with fatigue and he flew on by sheer force of will, knowing what would happen if he had to descend.

Gabe woke up and started blowing little spit bubbles, making explosive little *puh-puh* sounds. Logos' neck got wet with saliva. In the stillness of the night, the noise sounded like it could carry for miles. Logos put his hand over Gabe's mouth and strained his ears to listen for approaching wings, but heard nothing.

The wind was against him now, and he was close to exhaustion. He didn't think he could fly much farther without landing and resting, but that would be a last resort.

A sylvan does not admit to pain.

Logos forced himself not to think of the pain and struggled on.

Gabe started to coo. Logos tried unsuccessfully to hush him. He thought he heard faint wing beats behind him and glanced nervously over his shoulder, even though he knew he couldn't make out anything in the blackness. I must be getting close to Benefield Manor, he told himself. If I can just find the clearing! I don't feel any change in the air currents. Wait. Is that light ahead? He turned his head to study the light from his peripheral vision. It *was* a light. That must be Benefield Manor! "Hang on. We're almost there," he whispered to Gabe.

The words were no sooner out of his mouth, than he heard wings approaching fast. At this time of night, it could only be the night guard. He must've heard Gabe's little noises. Fear made Logos fly faster, even though his muscles burned in resentment. The guard was closing in fast.

I'm finished!, Logos thought, panicking, and then he felt a rush of warm air and realized that the giant rooftop of Benefield Manor must be directly below him. He lowered his head, tucked his wings in tight and dived toward a small light. When he could make out the rooftop, he opened his wings and charged into the forest of turrets and chimney pots, swerving right, then left. Behind him, Logos heard the guard brake sharply and swear.

With a shock, Logos recognized the voice. It wasn't Stebin. It was Eckles! Logos gained a little distance and then more as the obstacles forced Eckles to slow down to avoid running into a chimney.

Logos mind raced for help as though time didn't exist. He thought of trying to open the hatch, and at once discounted the idea. The hatch was kept locked because of the children. At the last possible moment, he folded his wings and rolled over the edge of the roof.

Craack! The air vibrated as Eckles braked hard, and Logos felt the air change as his relentless foe recklessly followed him over the edge.

Taking a calculated risk, Logos let himself free-fall, hoping to land on the balcony of his old room, but he missed and fell all the way to the ground floor, landing hard on the terrace. Picking himself up, he threw his body at the door and grabbed the latch, praying it wasn't locked. The latch turned in his hand and he fell through the door, slamming it backward into Eckles' face. He rolled, cushioning Gabe in his wings, his momentum carrying him halfway across the floor before he came to a stop, gasping for air. He said a silent prayer of thanks to the Goddess.

They were safe now. Eckles wouldn't dare enter a human's shelter. The whoosh from the downdraft of powerful wings confirmed Eckles' departure.

17

REFUGE

Logos realized three things simultaneously: He was lying on the library floor, Gabe was screaming in fright—or pain, Logos didn't know which—and the Benefields were looking down at him.

"Logos!" Lord Benefield exclaimed. "Are you all right?"

Logos stood up, unsteady on his feet. Blood dripped from his split lip, and his hands shook as he took Gabe out of his carrying sling. Lady Benefield took Gabe from him and examined him. "He's all right—nothing broken. He's just frightened. What happened?" she asked. "Who was that chasing you?"

"Eckles, and he almost caught me." Logos stretched his wings to make sure nothing was broken.

"You're in trouble at home." Lord Benefield said somewhat unnecessarily.

"Yes."

"Why?"

Logos couldn't meet Lady Benefield's eyes. "I was banned—because I'm changed."

Lady Benefield gave a choked little gasp.

"The Council condemned me to Flat-Top Mountain, and I would've gone willingly, but they wanted to quarantine Gabe there until he grew up. I couldn't let that happen, so I decided to try to escape."

"Would Eckles have harmed you?" Lord Benefield asked.

"Not on purpose. He'd just drag us back home."

"Could he do that" she asked.

"Oh, yes. He's extremely strong." Logos paused and then said almost apologetically, "May I stay with you? I don't have any place else to go."

Lady Benefield beamed. "Of course you may. We're delighted to have you back."

Her husband nodded. "I agree whole heartedly. You're welcome to live here as long as you want."

"Thank you," Logos said.

"You can have the same room again, if you wish," Lady Benefield said.

"That would be fine."

"I'll take Gabe to the nursery for you," she said. "Let me know if there is anything you need."

Logos leaned forward, his forehead furrowed. "Don't let anyone take Gabe outside. The guards might kidnap him."

"I won't let anything happen to him," Lady Benefield promised. "Now go get some rest."

That night, Logos slept once more in the grand bed, but he kept his balcony window closed and locked. He didn't think Eckles would enter a human dwelling, but he wasn't taking any chances.

***

Logos slept late and woke up stiff and sore. His muscles complained from the effort of standing up and dressing. Daring a quick look outside his balcony, he glanced up and saw a golden speck in the sky, which could only be a guard, so he went back inside and sat down at the desk to study.

Trying to make out the words in *The Odyssey* helped him keep his mind off Tamara, and he made a mental list of difficult words to ask Lord Benefield about.

In early afternoon, when Gabe grew fussy from hunger, the nursemaid carried him to Logos' room. The two hungry sylvans made do with the filtered sunlight coming through the window, but they had to feed for a much longer time than normal. Lady Benefield interrupted them when she knocked on Logos' door and invited him for dinner. "Gabe can go to the nursery with the other children," she said. "It's safe there. I've told the twins not to take Gabe outside to sun, and they understand the danger."

"All right," Logos said. He couldn't mope around forever, and he owed it to the Benefields to be sociable. He joined them for dinner, although he requested and was served his usual salad and steamed vegetables. Even though I am already contaminated, he thought, I will honor the Goddess by keeping The Great Command forever. I will never eat meat again.

Acting like it was their everyday fare, the Benefields ate only vegetables, too. This courtesy touched Logos, because he knew they normally ate meat or fish as their main course.

After dinner, they adjourned to the library where they settled into the comfortable chairs to talk over a glass of port, Lady Benefield joining them.

"Lord Benefield," Logos said, thinking back to his recent conversation with Evree. "Why do you have a wall around your house?"

"Back in the days of tribal feuds, one of my ancestors built it for protection against marauding bands of thieves."

Lady Benefield glanced sideways at Logos. "Nowadays, the wall is useful to keep out rowdy bands of angel-watchers."

Logos laughed. "No offense," he said, "but why do humans love to fight?"

Lord Benefield shrugged. "I don't know. I suppose it's just our nature, but you're so right—humans are always fighting over something." He set down his glass. "Don't sylvans ever wage war?"

"No," said Logos. "Although we do guard our trees and ropes from predators, including humans. To injure another creature is a violation of The Great Command. Anyone who commits an unnecessary act of violence is banished. Isn't violence against your religion, too?"

"Yes, of course," Lord Benefield said. "It's against the sixth commandment—thou shalt not kill—but it refers to killing other people, not animals. And we believe it's acceptable to kill to protect our loved ones or even in self-defense."

"How many commandments do you have?"

"Only ten," answered Lady Benefield.

"So many! Why isn't 'thou shalt not kill' the first commandment," said Logos. "It should be, since it's the most important."

"I guess God didn't think so," Lady Benefield said, laughing.

"Didn't God give you any rules about what you can eat?" Logos asked.

"Yes, he did," Lord Benefield said, stroking his beard as though he didn't know how to explain. "But only people of the Jewish faith still keep them."

"Why? Aren't God's rules important anymore?"

Lord Benefield squirmed in his chair. "No—or rather yes, of course they are…but—I mean, since we're not Jewish, we don't have to keep the old laws."

Logos' brow furrowed as he pondered this. *Sylvans had to keep the Goddess' law, he thought. How could humans pick and choose among their God's laws?* This viewpoint was very strange. No wonder humans had written whole books about philosophy.

"Logos," Lady Benefield said, her face stern. "The meat I fed you damaged you, didn't it?"

Logos glanced at her and then looked down.

"I need to know," she persisted.

Logos took a deep breath. "All right—yes, that's exactly what happened."

"How did you change? You look the same to me."

"You might not see any difference, but Tamara noticed right away. She said I smelled bad—oh, excuse me!—and she detected a slight difference in my eye color."

"Eye color? Why does that matter?"

"It's not the color that's important, it's the change of color. Unlike you humans, all sylvans have green eyes. When the Fall occurred, the first difference to show up in the fallen was the fading of their green eyes. They faded from green to blue or even gray, and very soon after that, they lost their white eye rings. The changes in their disposition showed up more gradually."

"What are your eye rings for?" Lady Benefield asked. "Do they give you better eyesight?"

"Rings don't have anything to do with vision. They're for measuring distance. Looking down from the air, everything looks the same, which makes it hard to estimate distance. We expand and contract our rings and measure the difference in the amount of light coming in. Position is something we sense, relating to the Earth's energy lines. We can feel them. Don't you?"

"I can't, but I've known a few dowsers who claim they can locate underground water. I wonder if it's all related. Have you noticed any change in your disposition?" Lady Benefield asked.

"Oh, yes. I'm much more emotional and more impulsive. I can't think as clearly, and it's a struggle to do what's right."

"So, they expelled you," Lady Benefield said. "Where would you have gone?"

"They were going to take me to Flat-Top Mountain to de-wing me."

"Cut off your wings? How terrible!" Lady Benefield exclaimed. She made a face and shuddered.

"They don't actually *remove* the wings," Logos explained. "They cut one of the ligaments so that the wing is useless, and the fallen can't fly from Flat-Top Mountain. I don't have a problem with the law, but I couldn't go along with quarantining Gabe."

"Is Gabe changing too?" Lady Benefield asked.

"No, thank the Goddess, he's fine, but the Council decided to play it safe."

"You mean sometimes you aren't sure if someone is corrupted or not?" Lady Benefield asked.

"That sounds odd, but it's true. We learned it gradually at the time of the Fall. Nowadays, when a sylvan is born to malvans, I'm present at his birth to make sure the malvana doesn't nurse him and contaminate him. He—for some strange reason, all malvan-born are male—is brought to the main colony and then adopted out. Once he reaches young adulthood, he's taken to Flat-Top Mountain for a full sun cycle of observation. We call this period 'The Trial'. Before I go on, you need to understand that the fallen are extremely irritating individuals—more like humans than sylvans."

Lord Benefield raised an eyebrow, and Logos blushed and apologized again. "I'm sorry. What I mean is that the fallen behave very aggressively. They tease, they bully, and they're always trying to pick a fight. Many of them eat meat and coax you to eat it. If the guards aren't watching them, they'll cram it down your throat. Their private behavior is …" Logos stopped, blushed and glanced apologetically at Lady Benefield.

"It's all right," she said. "You can say it."

"Let's just say it's unnatural. There aren't any sylvanas there."

"What happens to a poor sylvan undergoing The Trial?" Lord Benefield asked.

"The guards watch him to see how he reacts. If he starts fights, invariably, he goes on to change. If so, he is dewinged and must live out his life at Flat Top Mountain. If he stays calm and doesn't let the fallen goad him into fighting, he's brought back to be examined by the healer and to be questioned by the Council. If he passes their inspection, he's considered to be a full citizen and is allowed to stay."

"But, if a malvan-born sylvan never nurses and he doesn't eat meat, how could he be contaminated?" Lady Benefield asked.

"Ah, you bring up a curious point. No one knows why, but every once in a while, that occurs. We suspect that the baby is contaminated in the malvana's womb or during birth. It's a great tragedy when it happens." Logos paused and added. "I think that's why we malvan-born sylvans are never completely trusted—even those of us who pass the test."

"I still don't quite understand," Lady Benefield said. "Why wouldn't they let Gabe stay until he reached young adulthood?"

"He's a special case. A malvan-born sylvan has never been fed human milk, so the Council doesn't know what to expect. They don't want to take any chances."

Indignation changed Lady Benefield's face. "What a terrible way to treat an innocent child!" she exclaimed. "You made the right decision to run away."

"Definitely, although I almost got caught. At first, I thought Eckles heard Gabe cooing, but since I've had time to reflect, I think Eckles was looking for me. He was supposed to fly the night patrol, and Tomos changed the schedule at the last minute. He must've suspected something wasn't right. I hope Tomos doesn't get into trouble over this."

"Logos," Lady Benefield said in a gentle voice. "You haven't mentioned Tamara."

Logos dropped his eyes. "I called off our engagement. Our marriage is impossible now." He thought of the expression on Tamara's face when he told her, and swallowed back tears. Suddenly, he was terribly tired and wanted to be alone. He got to his feet, thanked his host and hostess for dinner, bowed and left for his room.

18

CONFINEMENT

The next day, Gabe was crabby from lack of sun. He refused to eat mashed peas or carrots, rolled them around in his mouth and pushed them out with his tongue. Logos didn't blame him. Vegetables were a poor substitute for sun. He walked out on the balcony. The sky was cloudless, so he could see for miles. He'd see a guard if he were up there. He decided he could take Gabe out on the rooftop safely—if he left the hatch open and stayed close to the entrance—and if he watched for golden specks in the sky— and if he listened for wing beats—and most important of all—if he didn't fall asleep.

While they were sunning, Logos heard the ivy rustle and jumped up in alarm, but then relaxed as Gilkenney hauled himself onto the rooftop. "You came back, you old rascal," Logos said, stroking the cat's throat. "Did Tamara send you?" Gilkenney rolled over to let Logos scratch his belly, and then rumbled a contented purr. Gabe grabbed a handful of his fur.

"I see your cat found you again," Lord Benefield said as he stepped out to join him. Benefield gazed around the sky. "Are you sure you're safe here?"

"Right now we are. Visibility is unobstructed."

"What about when the sky is cloudy? How fast can a sylvan drop down from inside a cloud?"

"Pretty fast," Logos admitted.

Lord Benefield wagged his finger. "So, on partly cloudy days, you won't be able to sun out here." He paused. "Would the guards land when I'm with you?"

"No. They don't want anything to do with humans. Tomos might, though."

"Then I'll ask one of my men to accompany you until we find a better solution." He paced back and forth, stroking his beard, his brow wrinkled in thought. He stopped as he looked at Lady Benefield's glass house and swung around to face Logos. "I have an idea. How about using Mary's plant nursery? Is the sun strong enough inside for you?"

"The light probably is sufficient, but just barely. I find that filtered sunlight is different from unfiltered sunlight," he explained. "The sun's rays are less filling somehow, as part of if the light is missing. The glass house does offer unobstructed light all day, so sunning inside it would be an improvement over moving from window to window inside the house. But if the guards see me there, they'll just stand outside the door and wait for me to come out. I'd be forced to yell for help, or pound on the floor until help came."

"And the nursery is right below you. With all the racket my children make, no one would ever hear you!"

They laughed, then Benefield snapped his fingers. "I know what. I'll build a hatch under the glass house, so you can enter and leave from the manor, and you won't have to go outside at all."

"That's a great idea," Logos said, "but it's way too much trouble."

Lord Benefield shook his head. "Nonsense. I'll look into it right away."

"One other thing," Logos said. "Since I'm going to live here, I want to earn my keep. Put me to work helping build it."

Eyes twinkling, Lord Benefield said, "All right, you can start by directing the construction project."

Lord Benefield hired a carpenter who promised to come the next day. He and Logos waited anxiously for him in the library, peering out the windows, but the man couldn't get to the gate because of the crowds. Word had got around that Logos was back. Beeks located the carpenter, pulled him through the crowd, locked the gate behind them and escorted him through the kitchen to Lord Benefield's library.

When the carpenter laid eyes on Logos, his mouth dropped open. "By God, the story's true then," he said, not taking his eyes off Logos. "You *do* have angels here."

"I assure you, I'm no angel," said Logos.

Lord Benefield laughed. "Meet Logos. He's in charge of the project."

"Come with me. I'll show you what we want done," Logos said, turning to leave the room.

The carpenter blanched. "Don't worry. He's harmless," Lord Benefield assured him.

When the carpenter still hesitated. Lord Benefield sighed and said, "I'll go with you."

"Isn't this a great view?" Logos asked the carpenter as they walked out onto the roof. "We can see the crowd real well from here."

The carpenter grinned. By the time Logos finished explaining what he wanted, the man had relaxed. He measured the area, estimated how much lumber he would need and left to visit the sawyer's shop to order the pieces.

Soon after the sawyer delivered the lumber, the manor had a burst of noisy activity as the carpenter sawed the wood, hammered the risers and treads into place, cut a hole under the glass house and built a hatch door. Logos helped, learning much about woodworking and tools. He admired the heavy metal tools, which were stronger than any he had ever seen. Gilkenney disappeared at the first smash of the hammer and didn't come near the house for the entire week.

After he completed the project, the carpenter told Logos, "You can be the first to walk up the stairs?" He grinned. "Or will you fly?"

"I'll walk. The steps are way too narrow to fly up," Logos said, missing the joke.

The carpenter laughed and packed away his tools. Then Logos walked him to the kitchen door.

"Goodbye. I've enjoyed meeting you and working with you," the carpenter said.

"Me, too. Safe flying," Logos said without thinking.

"What?"

"I mean good-bye." Logos said, holding out his hand.

Logos climbed up the stairs, entered the glass house, and gazed down at the weathered outbuildings, the huge barn and stables, the pastures spotted with grazing sheep. This was beginning to feel like home. If only Tamara were here, life would be perfect. He sighed. He knew it was useless to think such thoughts. He had to learn to live without her.

Logos took the Benefields up to inspect the new entrance to the glass house. Lady Benefield had to be helped up the stairs, because she had put on a lot of weight with her pregnancy. "What do you think?" Logos asked as they opened the hatch door and stepped inside the glass house.

"It's perfect," Lord Benefield said. "Now we can stop worrying about you."

"I love it, too," added Lady Benefield. "I won't have to walk halfway across the roof to take care of my plants." She nudged her husband. "Harold, why didn't you think of this sooner?"

***

The next day Logos took Gabe out to sun in the glass house for the first time. To help pass the time, Logos took *The Iliad* and practiced sounding out the words. Gabe thought Logos was talking to him and rewarded Logos with his first toothless grin.

As he read, Logos felt eyes on his back, and the hairs on the back of his neck stood up. He spun around to find a red-faced Eckles pressing both palms on the glass. There was an ugly, egg-shaped bump on his forehead. Logos stood up, uneasy. He hadn't heard Eckles fly up or land and he wondered how long he'd been watching.

Eckles pounded on the glass. Logos, afraid the glass would break, snatched up Gabe, and headed for the hatch.

"That's right—run, you coward!" Eckles shouted. "By the Goddess, I'll bring you back if it's the last thing I do." He turned and jumped into the sky.

Eckles' visit left Logos shaken, but he took some comfort in the thought that Eckles hadn't tried to break in. If he had, he would surely have caught them.

***

At dinner, as Lady Benefield and Logos watched Lord Benefield chase peas around his plate, Lady Benefield asked, "Logos, you've explained why sylvans don't eat meat, but what about other food? For example, what about fish?"

Logos set down his fork. "For such a simple command we live by, there are a great many interpretations. Some sylvans take it literally. They say we are kin to all living creatures, including plants, and insist the Goddess meant for us to live only on sunlight and water. Some believe the prohibition only applies to warm-blooded animals, and that we can eat cold-blooded animals, such as fish and seafood. Most of us eat fruits and vegetables only when we can't get enough sun."

"Other than meat, is there any evidence that diet makes a difference in your health?" Benefield asked, finally spearing a pea.

Logos knew that Lord Harold was tired of eating vegetables. He'd told the Benefields not to change their menu for him, however, they refused to set meat on the table. "Interestingly enough, what we eat does matter," he answered. "Vegetable eaters can argue all they like, but they can't dispute the fact that our longest-lived individuals—*and* the ones with the best memories—are the purists who live only on sunlight and water. Starvation somehow slows down the aging process. Some of them are well over a hundred years old and still vigorous."

Benefield choked down another forkful of peas. "Maybe it just seems like hundreds of years."

Logos laughed and then added, "We don't have as many centenarians as we used to. Keeping to a pure sun diet is difficult, now that sunlight has changed."

Lord Benefield's eyebrows shot up. "Sunlight has changed? How so?"

"Since the human population has increased so drastically, smoke has begun to obscure the sun. Sunlight contains fewer colors and provides less nutrition."

"I take it sylvans are eating more fruits and vegetables?" Lady Benefield asked.

"Yes. Few sylvans live on sunshine alone. Most of us can't stand to go hungry."

"Where do you grow your plants?" asked Lady Benefield. "On Flat Top Mountain?"

"That's correct. Over the years, we've built terraced gardens. They're quite extensive now, and they grow enough to supply all the colonies."

"How very interesting," Lady Benefield said. "I never knew anything lived up there but seagulls."

"You wouldn't," Logos said. "You can't see the top from below, and no human has ever scaled the walls."

"You're right about that," Lord Benefield said, stabbing his fork into the air for emphasis. "When I was a young man, I hiked over there intending to climb the walls. They're unscalable—not just vertical, but slightly overhung, and almost completely smooth, as though someone planed them ..." He shot a questioning look at Logos whose face wore a smug expression.

Dropping his fork on his plate, Lord Benefield leaned forward. "You don't mean to say you sylvans chiseled those walls smooth?"

"We did," Logos said. This happened way before my time, though. When The Fall occurred, we needed a place to keep the fallen where they couldn't get away, so the hoverers smoothed the sides so nobody could climb down. We lugged the rock chips to the top and used them to chink the rock walls for the raised gardens. We've grown our plants there for many generations."

"What would you do if the volcano blew up?" Lord Benefield asked.

"That would be a disaster. Not only would we need a new place to grow food, but we'd also have to relocate the malvans and the fallen. We can't go south because humans live there. We could move to the far north, but silkiron trees don't grow there. We'd have to change our lifestyle drastically, since we rely on the trees for so many things. We spin silkiron fibers into threads for ropes for the platforms and huts." Logos bit his lip as he realized he had said too much.

"You could go to that western world you told me about," Lord Benefield suggested.

"That's too far away," Logos said, darting a look to see if he were serious. "And who would take care of the malvans?"

"You could build an ark, like Noah," Lady Benefield said, with a smile on her face.

"Who's Noah?" Logos asked, "And what's an ark?"

"An ark is a very large boat," she explained. "Long ago when it rained for forty days and forty nights, and the whole Earth was flooded ..."

"That's a myth," Logos interrupted. "The Earth was never flooded."

Looking bewildered, Lady Benefield stopped speaking.

"I'm sorry," Logos said. "Please go on."

"Noah rescued the animals by building an ark and taking aboard two of each species until the water receded and they came out onto dry land."

"That's a good story," Logos said, "but we couldn't build an ark even if we wanted to. We don't know how."

"You could learn," Lord Benefield said.

"That's ridiculous," Logos said and then caught himself. Why was he being rude and disagreeing with everything? Instead, he said, "I'm sorry. Yes. We could learn. I've learned some basic woodworking skills here myself."

19

TAMARA'S FIRST DECISION

The evening before Logos was to be dewinged at Flat Top Mountain, Tamara had gone to her room early but stayed up all night on her knees begging the Goddess to help Logos. In the morning, there was a knock on the outside door. She heard her father talking to one of the guards and heard Logos' name mentioned. She threw on her clothes and went to him. He said, "Tamara, I have something to tell you. Logos and Gabe are missing. Evidently, Logos ran away in the night. Eckles chased him but couldn't catch him. He's gone back to the human shelter. He scrutinized her closely as he spoke. "You don't know anything about this, do you?" he asked. His tone suggested he thought she did.

Tamara shook her head. "No, I don't, Father." Her chin shot up, and she fixed a defiant look on him. "But I'm glad he got away."

"Council is meeting to decide what course of action to take," he replied, his lips set, his eyes disapproving. He turned and walked away from her.

Tamara felt his disappointment keenly. As soon as she could escape to her room, she fell on her knees to thank the Goddess and to renew her prayers for Logos' and Gabe's safety. She refused to sun and turned her nose up at the fresh fruit her mother brought to tempt her. That afternoon, when her father came back from emergency council, he called her and her mother together and said, "Council decided to post guards to watch the human shelter. Eckles saw Logos in some sort of transparent house on top of the roof. He asked for permission to break into it and seize him!"

"Did he really?" Tamara's mother said.

"Yes. When Evree refused, Eckles argued with him! Evree said, 'You're acting like one of the flagits!' Eckles shut up in a hurry."

Tamara's mother laughed, but Tamara, lost in thought, didn't. The transparent house must be Lady Benefield's glass house that had so fascinated Logos. He had suggested that maybe the humans would teach him the secret of making glass, so they could build glass houses on Flat Top Mountain. Now, that would never happen.

Tamara's anxiety was eased now that Logos was safe, but she missed Logos and Gabe and remained quiet and withdrawn. She moped around distracted, only going out to sun when her parents insisted. Cinsha came by to talk and coaxed her back to work. But working with children, a job she loved, provided little consolation. Tomos found many occasions to be with Tamara. He joined her on the community platform to sun, flowers in hand. He met her after he was off duty and flew her home. He brought her fragrant berries fresh-picked from the gardens at Flat-Top Mountain. However, when he asked her to go flying with him, she refused. "Can't we just be friends?" she asked.

"I *am* your friend," said Tomos. "I'm your best friend. I'd like to be more."

"I'm not ready yet," she replied.

Tamara's parents never missed an opportunity to praise Tomos and tell her how much they liked him. Her grandmother reminded her that time heals all heartaches. Well-meaning friends told her that she had to accept the fact that Logos was gone forever and get on with her life. Logos would agree with them. Under this unrelenting pressure, Tamara eventually agreed to go flying with Tomos, and eventually said yes to an engagement, thinking she would forget Logos and learn to love Tomos.

A moon-cycle went by, then two. The more time passed, the more she missed Logos. Her mother wove Tamara's intricately patterned wedding robe, and one day as they were embroidering it, her mother casually remarked, "We have to hurry up and finish this. Blessing Day is coming up soon."

Startled, Tamara pricked her finger. She felt as though she had awakened from a trance. Oh, Goddess! What had she done? She couldn't marry Tomos. She was still in love with Logos!

It was at that moment when Tamara first thought about running away.

Initially, she dismissed the idea. Like most females, she wasn't a strong flyer. Even if she left in the middle of the night, the thought of which frightened her to death, she had little or no chance of getting past the guard, and if she did, she couldn't fly to Benefield Manor without needing to land and rest several times. On the ground, she would be in danger from wild animals and possibly humans. She shivered at the thought. Then too, she only knew where Benefield Manor was located in relation to the malvan cave, so her chances of finding Logos were slim indeed.

But the idea haunted her. The more she pondered it, and the closer her wedding date got, the more escape seemed to be the only answer. Logos would tell her it was a stupid idea—dangerous and futile. He'd broken off their engagement and advised her to forget him and marry Tomos. He'd probably send her home.

On the other hand, her directional memory was good. If she flew to the malvan cave first, she could find Benefield Manor from there. She thought of when she had visited the dark underground cave—remembered the smoke and the odor of burning flesh—and shuddered. The malvans had been kind to her, but Tomos had been with her then. Did she really want to go back alone? If only she had someone to ask for advice, but whom? Her friends would be aghast at the idea. Tomos? Never! Her mother? Impossible! She had no one to turn to for help.

She considered her options over and over and always came to the same conclusion. She must get to Benefield Manor. What was the worst the guards could do if they caught her? Clip her wings? Feathers grow back. Send her to Flat-Top Mountain? She—a sylvana, and a councilor's daughter? Not likely. Yes, she would leave. But how?

The next afternoon when Tomos mentioned preparations for the upcoming Blessing Day ceremony, Tamara knew immediately how she would get away. Of course! Why hadn't she thought of this before?

The Blessing Day ceremony, the biggest event of the year, was held at Flat-Top Mountain where sylvans from both colonies gathered once a year to watch the sunrise and to thank the Goddess for all her blessings. She wouldn't have to worry about getting past the guards because they would be busy keeping the fallen away. The guards didn't need to patrol the sky because the mountain was accessible only by flight. Slipping away from the large crowds would be easy.

She was fairly confident that she could find the malvan cave again. However, since she'd have to stop and rest often, she'd need some defense against predators. At work, she'd often watched the children load their slings and shoot silkiron cones at each other. She joined in the game and practiced until her aim grew true. She secretly glided down to the forest floor to search for small stones, and then hid them in her carrying pouch.

Blessing Day was actually a two-day event. The entire colony left on the eve and camped overnight in order to be in place as the sun left the Goddess' bower and rose to begin the first arc exactly centered between two great stone columns whose origin was shrouded in mystery. Sylvans couldn't have moved the stones, so they believed the Goddess herself must've set them there. After prayers, couples exchanged marriage vows and then everyone celebrated with music and dance. In the afternoon at the closing ceremony, a youth recited the story of The Fall, so that the children would learn and remember. Then they all renewed their pledge to refrain from animal products. Tamara had been the one chosen to tell the tale the year she turned thirteen.

The afternoon before the big day, Tamara dressed in her best embroidered clothes but wore her plain flying outfit underneath. "Are you ready, Tamara?" her mother called. "Tomos and Eckles are here with our carrying basket."

Folding her cloak, Tamara stashed it in a large bag.

"Ready, Mother," she sang out.

Tamara's mother smiled. "I'm glad to see you so cheerful. I'm sure you'll be happy with Tomos."

"Yes, Mother," Tamara said.

Tomos was resplendent in his embroidered clothes and new headband, now with several strands of well-earned silkiron which Tamara had interwoven for him. He had oiled his feathers which gleamed in the sunshine. He smiled and greeted her and her mother with a deep bow. They didn't speak on the trip over. When they arrived, Tamara kissed her mother and thanked Eckles for escorting her, and told Tomos, "I won't see you until the ceremonies tomorrow. I'm staying with Cinsha tonight. A last night with my girlfriends."

"All right," he said, not sounding surprised. "I'll be with my friends, too."

"Good-bye," she said, kissing him lightly on the cheek.

"Good-bye?" he repeated. "I'll see you first thing in the morning." He smiled and touched his cheek as though he wanted to protect the kiss. As she watched him fly off to join his bachelor friends, suddenly she felt so guilty for deceiving him.

Tamara told her mother she was spending the night with Cinsha, but she let Cinsha believe she was staying with her parents. That way, neither of them would look for her until the next morning. She was amazed how easy it was to lie and wondered if she really were a pure sylvan.

20

TAMARA'S SECOND DECISION

Tamara had to leave Flat Top Mountain immediately, because sylvans would be arriving all evening. She waited until her mother ran off to talk to a friend, then she dodged behind a boulder. Slipping off her ceremonial clothes, she folded them, laid them on the ground, and hid them underneath a pile of flat rocks, cringing as she thought of the amount of work that her mother had put into their creation. She had intended to leave her cloak behind, too, but at the last moment, she decided it might be useful as a blanket. She looked around to make sure no one was watching, walked to the edge of the mountain, jumped off, glided, opened her wings, and flew away at maximum speed.

To her chagrin, her burning wing muscles soon forced her to slow down. She took a quick glance over her shoulder, fully expecting to see strong-winged guards coming after her, but she was alone in the sky. No one had noticed her leave. She thanked the Goddess and checked on the position of the sun to get her bearings. Like all sylvanas, she'd never taken navigational classes, because females didn't need navigation skills. Still, every sylvan, both male and female, had innate directional skills. Flat-Top

Mountain lay behind her. She triangulated her eye rings with the Earth's energy lines, and adjusted her flight path to fly slightly west of south.

She'd never flown alone out of sight of New Solari, and she was dreadfully afraid. Beneath her, an unending blanket of green spread out in all directions. The forest below was full of dangers, and she had a long distance to fly. An updraft supported her for a while, allowing her to glide and rest her wings, but it began dragging her off course, and she reluctantly had to change course.

Flat Top Mountain became smaller and smaller until it was a dot and then disappeared, and she had only her inner bearings. She flew farther than she'd ever flown before, and although she hadn't traveled half the distance, she already needed to stop and rest. Looking for a place to land, she spotted a lake with a wide beach, circled once to check that no humans or beasts lurked in the vicinity and then landed. She knelt down by the shore to drink and to refill her water carrier with the clear water. Since there weren't any tall trees nearby, she sat down underneath a willow tree and leaned against its cool trunk. The combination of the birds singing and the gentle swaying of the branches proved hypnotic. She closed her eyes—just for a moment.

The snap of a twig awakened her. Charging straight at her with his head lowered was a huge boar. She jumped to her feet and leaped into the air as the beast lunged at her. The downstroke of her wing cracked him on his snout. He swung his tusks from side to side, searching for his prey with his beady, blood-red eyes. When he failed to find her, he snorted and pawed the dirt.

Heart pounding, Tamara quickly gained altitude, took her bearings and resumed her flight, thanking the Goddess for saving her life, and berating herself for being so careless as to fall asleep on the ground. She'd lost her water carrier, too, but she wasn't going back for it. The sun hung near the tree line. Soon it would pass into the eighth arc and then sink into the Goddess' bower. What if she couldn't find the malvans before dark? To return home was unthinkable, and she didn't want to spend a night alone in the woods, even in a tree top. She thought of New Solari where guards protected the colony from humans and other predators. Other than those few heart-stopping times when a child had tumbled off the infants' platform, and she had to fly down to rescue it, she'd never had to worry about predators. When the sylvanas went to the forest floor to gather silkiron cones, they were always accompanied by guards. Now, for the first time in her life, she was alone and vulnerable. She quenched her rising panic and prayed for help.

Twice more, fatigue forced her down, but she had learned her lesson. She sat where she could monitor her surroundings, and she didn't allow herself to close her eyes even for a moment.

Only at dusk did she reluctantly accept the awful inevitability of holing up in the woods for the night. Circling to locate a secure place, she spotted a dead tree with a wide fork near its top, and landed. Here, she could sleep well above the wilderness floor, safe from most predatory animals. First thing in the morning, she would fly high and look for the mound. She felt certain she was near the area she had visited with Tomos.

She curled up in the crotch of the tree, and had almost managed to get comfortable when she heard desperate screaming and the sound of something heavy charging through the brush. She leaned over the branch to see what was causing the commotion, and gasped as she saw a malvan child running toward a pile of rocks. He was closely pursued by a bear and couldn't possibly reach safety. Without thinking, she threw herself out of the tree, loading her slingshot and firing as her feet hit the ground. It was a lucky shot. The sharp stone hit the bear's sensitive nose, stopping him in his tracks. He screamed in pain, reared on his hind legs, and then spun about and scrambled off, while Tamara pelted his backside with more stones.

Trembling, Tamara looked around for the child. He stared down at her from on top of the rock pile. Then coming from behind her, she heard deep-throated guttural sounds. The boy returned the grunts. Tamara jumped onto a branch and watched as an adult malvan male ran up, grabbed the boy, and alternately hugged him and yelled at him. The boy pointed to Tamara and flapped his arms. When the adult glanced up at her, Tamara thought she recognized him as one of the malvans she had seen on her previous trip with Tomos.

"Hello," Tamara said. The adult raised his hand in greeting and waved her down.

Tamara glided down feeling proud of herself. She had been right about the cave being close by.

The adult, who Tamara decided must be the boy's father, made some low grunting sounds and put his huge paw over his heart. Tamara thought he was thanking her for saving his son, so she smiled and said, "You're welcome." The malvan shoved the boy toward a rocky outcropping and signaled for Tamara to follow. She pinned her wings close to her body and threaded her way through the dense brush and piles of rock. At the foot of a cliff, the adult pulled aside thorny bushes and rolled a stone away, revealing a low entrance. The boy scrambled in, and his father gestured for Tamara to enter. Tamara hesitated. She hated their tunnels, and even though she knew she had to go in, some unreasonable dread held her back. When the malvan repeated the gestured somewhat impatiently, she dropped down on her hands and knees and crawled in after the child. The malvan pulled the stone to cover the entrance and followed behind them.

The small tunnel soon enlarged, allowing her to stand upright, and eventually, the passage entered a cavern which Tamara recognized was the same one she'd visited with Tomos. They must have come in from a different entrance. She glanced around the cave anxiously for a sylvan, and then remembered with relief that most sylvans were at Flat-

Top Mountain for Blessing Day. A few had stayed home to take care of the ill and aged. She wondered who would take Logos' place as mediator to the malvans.

As she entered, every head turned toward her. The malvans and malvanas started growling and pointing. Tamara fought the urge to turn and run, but then Geera came forward, showing her teeth and making low chuck-chuck noises of welcome. She took Tamara by the hand and led her past the gawkers and over to her stone-ringed hearth. Tamara stopped and stared in undisguised revulsion at a young pig, head and all, roasting over a fire. Geera motioned for her to sit down on a log. Tamara sat and watched, both fascinated and disgusted as the fat dripped off the dead pig's body into the coals, and the skin blackened and cracked, the odor filling her nose and nauseating her. Behind Geera's hearth, four other fires held similar fare. Evidently, the tribe had recently conducted a very successful hunt. The smoke wafted upwards and blended into the darkness of the ceiling. Tamara wondered who provided Geera with food since she lost her mate. Did females hunt with the males? She'd have to remember to ask Logos, if—no—*when*—she saw him again.

Every once in a while, Geera turned the carcass on a spit until the skin became crisp all over, and then pulled the meat off to the side of the fire to cool. Sitting down next to Tamara, she made throaty sounds and gestures in an obvious attempt to communicate.

"I'm trying to find Logos," Tamara said.

Geera's eyes flashed with recognition. She mimicked rocking motions with her arms.

"Yes, that's right, Logos," Tamara said, repeating the gesture. "He's at Benefield Manor. Can someone take me to him?" Geera shrugged. Tamara wasn't sure what she meant. Perhaps she didn't understand or maybe she thought no one would be foolish enough to risk his life for her. Geera signaled for Tamara to remain where she was and walked over to a neighboring stone ring to talk to another couple.

They both shook their heads. Geera appeared to argue with them and then gave up and stomped off to several other hearths with the same results. Eventually, Geera reached the hearth that belonged to the parents of the boy that Tamara had rescued. The male nodded right away, however, his mate grabbed him as though to hold him back and shook her head vehemently. Tamara wondered if anyone knew where Logos was—or if they knew where Benefield Manor was for that matter. Maybe she'd have to find him herself.

It had been an exhausting day. Tamara's eyelids grew heavy, and she stifled a yawn. Would it be rude to lay down to nap? Her head fell forward, and she snapped it upright. Geera returned, sat down and touched the roasted pig to test if it was cool enough to eat. She jerked her hand back. While she waited, she offered Tamara her skin pouch full of water. Tamara took a drink, hoping the water was pure. Geera kept glancing at the far end of the cave, as though she was looking for someone.

As soon as the meat had cooled to her satisfaction, Geera cut off a slice of meat and handed it to Tamara almost apologetically, as if to say, "I know you won't eat this, but I have to offer it to be hospitable."

This was the answer! Making an instant decision, Tamara took the greasy, smelly meat, tore off a bite-sized piece, squeezed her eyes shut, and in one quick motion, shoved the meat in the back of her throat and swallowed it without chewing. Her body gave an involuntary shudder of revulsion, and her stomach heaved. She clasped her belly and willed herself to keep the food down. As the wave of nausea passed, she opened her eyes, surprised that—other than the smoky taste in her mouth and the greasy coating on her tongue—she didn't feel any different. But she *was* profoundly different. She'd been contaminated like the fallen—like Logos. She could never go home again. A sense of overwhelming loss and shame hit her. "Oh, Goddess! What have I done?" she breathed out.

Geera, surprised but obviously pleased that Tamara had tried her food, smiled and offered her some more. Tamara gave a slight shake of her head, lay down on the furs and closed her eyes again, trying not to vomit. Geera pulled a fur over Tamara and tiptoed off.

As she slept, Tamara had nightmares of being chased by the fallen. She awoke with a start when Geera shook her by the shoulders and then reached forward and tenderly wiped some tears from her eyes, all the while making a crooning sound eerily reminiscent of the sound that sylvanas use to comfort a child. Tamara sat up, unsure if she'd actually eaten meat or only dreamed it. As her head cleared, she saw the grease on her fingers and tasted the meat. It was all true. She had broken The Great Command. She wondered how long it would be before she began to change, and whether or not she would recognize the changes in herself. Logos had said that he felt himself changing almost immediately.

As she pondered these things, another malvan entered. Geera called out to him, and he walked over to her. Tamara thought he might be Jarat. Tomos had talked with this malvan at their previous visit, and Logos had told her that he had a malvan friend named Jarat who understood sylvan language better than most malvans. Tamara stood, raised her hand in greeting and asked, "Are you Jarat?"

The malvan nodded. Tamara said, "I need to find Logos. He's gone back to Benefield Manor. Can you tell me the way? Do you understand me?"

Jarat nodded and left to confer with the other males. After much gesticulating, grunting, and head shaking, he returned with the father of the boy whom Tamara had saved, motioned for her to join them and then headed for the exit. They want to leave right away? Tamara thought in surprise, looking at Geera for confirmation. Geera gave a brief nod and showed her teeth in what Tamara took to be encouragement. Tamara hugged Geera goodbye and turned to follow the malvans.

They left by the main passage, the one Tamara remembered from her first visit, and set out at a fast lope through the woods, as though they could see in the dark. She tried to stay close to them, although she kept tripping over logs and rocks and falling. Her lightweight landing sandals weren't built for hiking, and soon tore and fell off. She cut her foot on a sharp rock and emitted an involuntary cry of pain. The malvans stopped and exchanged grunts. To Tamara's surprise, Jarat picked her up and placed her on his back. Tamara threw her arms around him, folded her wings as compact as possible and tucked her head into his furry neck to avoid being slapped by branches. The malvans speeded up to a clumsy run. They seemed to be following some sort of a path, and they acted as though they knew exactly where they were going. Tamara watched nervously for first light. She didn't know how long she had slept at Geera's hearth, and since the stars weren't visible through the thick tree canopy she couldn't estimate the time of day. She only knew it wasn't wise for the malvans to be out after daylight. She thought of Geera's mate being killed by humans. By daybreak, all malvans needed to be underground in the safety of their home.

Rocked by their rhythmic movements, Tamara nodded off, lurched sideways and almost fell off. A huge paw reached back to hold her on, and she sank into sleep again. She awoke again as the malvan lifted her over his head and gently set her down on her bare feet. She was dismayed to find that the sun was already well into the first arc. Back on Flat Top Mountain, Tomos and her mother would be looking for her. They stood at the border of a field. Beyond she made out several buildings, one of them a large house surrounded by a wall.

"Is that where Logos lives?" Tamara asked.

Jarat nodded.

"I can go on my own from here. Thank you for helping me," Tamara said.

They showed their teeth and then stayed as though waiting for her to leave.

She smiled. They should be home in the protection of their cave, but they wanted to be sure she was safe before they left. "Good-bye, and thank you again," she said, reaching up to give each a quick hug. She jumped into the air and flew across the clearing to the manor, forgetting that Logos had told her there was always a crowd of humans hanging around. A shout arose, "Look! Look over there! One's coming!"

Startled, Tamara quickly gained altitude and landed on the great roof. She walked among the tall towers and chimneys which were exactly as Logos had described and found what seemed to be a doorway of some sort, constructed of thin, even strips of wood. However, thousands of sun cycles of tradition prevented her from opening the door, let alone entering a human house.

Unsure of what to do next, she looked around at the rest of the roof. Farther down sat a small building, built out of a transparent material. The rising sun's rays reflected off the one side turning it into a blazing sheet of gold. This must be the little house in which Logos sunned—the one Eckles had asked for permission to break into. She remembered Logos saying that the walls were made of a clear material called glass. Going over to the strange house, she tapped on a pane to assure herself it was solid, and peeked through, ready to flee if she as much as glimpsed a human. The room was empty except for several rows of plants on tables. This obviously was Lady Benefield's plant house, the one Logos admired and wanted to replicate on Flat Top Mountain.

She was hungry, but the sun was still too low to provide adequate nutrition, so she sat down next to the glass house. Gilkenney startled her when he appeared on the roof. He sat beside her, rolled onto his back and began to purr. Tamara stroked his spotted belly. "Gilkenney, I'm sure glad to see you. If you're here, that means Logos must be nearby." Gilkenney purred louder and exercised his claws in the air. Tamara curled up around him, closed her eyes and fell asleep.

21

BLESSING DAY

When Logos came up to greet the sun on Blessing Day, and saw Tamara pressed against the glass, he didn't believe his eyes. Throwing caution to the winds, he unlocked the door and ran to her side. "Tamara," he whispered, touching her hair tentatively as though afraid she would disappear.

"Logos!" She sat up and threw her arms around him.

"What are you doing here?" he asked. He drew in his breath sharply as he noticed her bleeding foot. "Barefoot! And you're hurt!"

She clung to him. "It's nothing—just a scratch."

"We need to get inside," Logos said, pulling her to her feet. "It's not safe out here. The guards might spot us."

Tamara smiled. "Silly, they're all at Flat Top Mountain for Blessing Day."

"Of course," Logos said, but he took her arm, pulled her inside the glass house and locked the door behind him anyway. He turned to face her. "How did you get here?"

"I slipped away from the crowd at Flat Top Mountain last evening and flew to the malvan's cave—the one Tomos took me to when you had your accident. The malvans brought me here this morning."

Logos looked at her with disbelief. "You flew all that way by yourself, and you managed to find the malvans? Thank the Goddess you're alive!" He hugged her, and then held her at arms length. "I'm glad to see you, but you know you can't stay."

"I'm never going back."

"You must return. You're young. You should marry and have children."

"I want to be with you."

"You don't know what you're saying. You don't know what it's like to live here. Sure, the humans are wonderful, but I feel like I'm in a cage. I can't fly—I can't even step outside alone for fear the guards will capture me. They fly by here every day, hoping to catch me outside. With you here, they'll redouble their efforts. Your father will order every available guard out to search for you. He'll never rest until he gets you back."

Tamara took his hands. "That's true, but I can't go back … I have something to tell you—something terrible. Don't hate me."

"Never!"

"I knew that you'd send me back, and that Father would search everywhere for me. Last night, when I was with the malvans, I suddenly realized the only way I could be *with* you was to be *like* you." She hesitated and blurted out, "Logos, I ate meat."

Logos gaped at her for several moments, stunned. Finally, he asked, "On purpose?"

She nodded and dropped her eyes.

"I don't know what to say."

"Say you still love me."

"Of course I love you."

"Will you marry me?" Tamara asked.

Logos stared at her. "You know the fallen are forbidden to marry. We could never risk having children. They might be malvan."

"Would that be so terrible?" Tamara asked. "The malvans are good people. Besides we have Gabe. He will be our son …" She stopped. Logos was staring at her again. "Logos, say something!"

"I—I," Logos stammered. "I don't know what to say," he repeated.

"Say you'll marry me."

"Shouldn't I be the one to propose?"

"You still can."

Logos folded her in his wings. "Will you be my wife?"

"Yes." She took his face in her hands and kissed him. When they stopped to catch their breath, she glanced toward the east and said, "Look, the sun is over the treetops now."

Kneeling, they chanted the prayer of thanksgiving for the life-giving rays of the sun as the Goddess poised to take flight on her longest journey over the Earth.

"Do you think she'll forgive me?" Tamara asked.

"I think so. She knows you did it out of love."

"There is something I have to tell you."

"What else?"

Tamara took a deep breath. "After you left, I got engaged to Tomos."

Logos raised his eyebrows.

"I know now that I should never have said yes, but my parents told me it was what you would want, and it seemed like the right thing to do. Then one day I woke up and realized I couldn't marry Tomos, because I was still in love with you. That's when I decided to leave New Solari. Poor Tomos. He's been so kind and patient, and I left him on the eve of our marriage." She bit her lip. "I'm sorry, Logos."

"You don't need to apologize. After all, I'm the one who urged you to marry him." He kissed her forehead.

"Let's get married now," Tamara said suddenly.

"What? Right now?"

"Yes—on Blessing Day. The traditional day. The most auspicious time."

"Alone, without family—without ceremony?"

"I've cut myself off from my parents forever, and you don't have any family," she reminded him."

"All right then," said Logos. "But first, let's go inside. I may not have a sylvan family, but I have a human family now. I want you to meet them, and I want to invite them to the wedding."

Tamara drew back. "I'm afraid of them."

Logos laughed. "You have nothing to fear from them. Besides, if you're going to live here, you need to get used to them."

"Can I see Gabe first?" Tamara asked. "I'm anxious to see how much he's grown. Do you think he'll remember me?"

"Maybe. He's changing every day. He rolls over, he can push himself up on his arms, and he has the cutest little crooked grin."

Throwing open the hatch, Logos led her down the steps and into the house. Tamara clung to his arm and glanced behind as though calculating the distance to escape.

"Don't worry," Logos said, chuckling. "This is just a house, although granted, a much larger and grander one than any sylvan has."

They walked down the hall and into the nursery. The twins were sitting on the floor playing peek-a-boo with Gabe. When they saw Tamara, they stood up and stared open-mouthed. Gabe grinned and held up his arms to Tamara to be picked up.

"You do remember me," Tamara said, scooping him up and kissing him. Gabe gurgled and grinned.

"Who's *she?*" the twins asked Logos.

"This is Tamara, my intended, soon to be my wife. Tamara these are the Benefield twins, Penny and Helen. Despite their great height, they're only ten years old."

"Hello," Tamara said, bowing.

Penny and Helen imitated her bow, making Tamara smile.

"This is baby Louise," Logos said, picking up the child from the crib and handing her to Tamara, then grabbing onto her as Tamara almost dropped her.

"She's beautiful," Tamara said, struggling to hold the child and then shifting the weight to her hip.

Tamara and I are getting married today," Logos told the twins. "Would you like to come to the wedding?"

"Oh, yes!" the twins said in unison. They looked at each other, squealed, grabbed each others arms, and jumped around in a circle.

Tamara smiled at their enthusiasm. "Come on," Logos said, pulling her by the hand. "Let's go downstairs and meet our hosts." They put down the baby and walked out into the hall, trailed by the excited twins.

When Logos and Tamara walked into the library, Lord and Lady Benefields' mouths dropped open, they got to their feet and rushed over. "Is this who I think it is?" Lady Benefield asked Logos.

"Yes, this is Tamara, my wife-to-be."

"They're getting married today," Helen blurted out.

"Wonderful! Congratulations!" Lord Benefield exclaimed. Lady Benefield hugged them both.

"You can get married in our chapel," Lady Benefield said.

"Thank you," Logos said, "but we need to be married outside in the sun for the Goddess' blessing."

"Very well. Do you want us to fetch a priest?" asked Lady Benefield.

"We don't need an religious leaders, we marry each other," Logos explained. "You'll come won't you? We've already invited the children. Do you suppose the men who rescued Gabe and me would like to come, too?"

"Oh, yes," Lady Benefield replied. "*Everyone* will want to come."

Lord Benefield left to round up his servants. His wife called for hot water and treated the cut on Tamara's foot.

When she had finished bandaging it, she stood up and asked shyly, "May I fix your hair for you, too?"

Tamara smiled, let down her coiled braids and began to unbraid them.

Logos watched as Lady Benefield combed the tangles out of Tamara's hair, and brushed it until it shone. When she had finished, Tamara removed her golden cloak from her bag and Logos fastened it around her shoulders. "You look so beautiful," he said in awe.

After everyone had gathered, they all walked out on the roof where the sun was now shining strong, and formed a circle around Logos and Tamara to watch the first sylvan wedding ever witnessed by humans.

Holding hands, and gazing into each other's eyes, Tamara and Logos chanted their ancient vows of love and faithfulness. As their voices died down and they kissed, their friends applauded and cheered.

"How beautiful," Lady Benefield said, wiping tears from her cheeks. "I feel like I just married off a son."

"Me, too," Lord Benefield said. He turned to his men, "Since today is such a special occasion, you may all have the rest of the day off. Smitty, go to the cellar and bring up a cask of wine."

The men cheered, causing Tamara to step closer to Logos. He laughed and put his arm around her waist. "You're in for a treat—your first wine."

As the women kissed Tamara and wished her happiness, and the rough-looking farmhands bowed shyly, hats in hand, to welcome and congratulate her, Tamara drank some wine and soon lost her fear of humans. Everyone laughed when she giggled and said, "The wine makes me feel like I couldn't fly straight."

The cask was emptied, and another one was brought up. As the sun grew hotter, the guests drifted away. Lord and Lady Benefield escorted Logos and Tamara to the safety of the glass house and left with reluctant children in tow.

Alone at last, the newlyweds sipped wine and talked, Tamara asking questions about the people she had met.

Unexpectedly, someone rapped sharply on the glass, making them both jump. They turned and found Tomos standing on the other side of the wall, still wearing his ceremonial tunic, his face stormy.

"Tamara, come out of there," he ordered.

"No," Tamara said in a strong voice. "I'm not coming out. I'm staying here."

"You must come home. Your parents are frantic with worry."

"Tell them I'm all right, and that I'm not going back—ever."

"Why not? It's our wedding day. Why did you run away? "

"Logos and I are married."

Tomos turned pale. "M-m-married?" he stammered out. "But—you're engaged to me."

"I'm so sorry Tomos," Tamara said. "I didn't mean to lead you on, and I apologize for leaving without telling you—but I couldn't. You wouldn't have let me go."

"You married a fallen sylvan? —a flagit?"

"Don't call him that!" Tamara snapped.

"What am I going to tell your father?" Tomos asked.

"Tell him the truth."

"He'll never accept it. Neither will I. You're coming home with me."

"Tamara is my wife now, and she's staying," Logos said, struggling to keep his voice level.

Tomos glared at Logos, his face red. He pressed both hands against the glass and shouted, "When I catch you outside—and I will—I'll drag you to Flat-Top Mountain where you belong with the rest of your miserable kind. I'll de-wing you myself."

"We'll see about that!" Logos shouted.

Tomos raised his fist, and for an awful moment, Logos thought Tomos was going to smash the glass, but then he turned and jumped into the sky, his powerful downdraft rattling the glass panes.

Logos pulled Tamara toward him and found she was shaking. "Don't worry," he told her. "Tomos is powerless here. We have each other, Gabe, and good friends. Everything will be all right."

22

ADAPTING

Human culture seemed very strange to Tamara, but she watched and learned and tried hard to make herself useful to Lady Benefield who was already getting huge and ungainly in her pregnancy.

"I think I'm carrying twins again," she told Tamara. "They run in my family. For Harold's sake, I hope one is a boy. We already have three girls, and I know he'd like a son and heir."

"Then I hope so, too," Tamara said.

When Tamara wasn't with Lady Benefield, she helped Mrs. Hogue in the nursery. She entertained the Benefield's baby, marveling at her weight, and occasionally took care of all the children, so Mrs. Hogue could visit her sister. The Benefield children loved Tamara, and Gabe's eyes followed her around the room.

Occasionally, Tamara joined Logos in the classroom. He had already become an accomplished reader and was perfecting his penmanship under Lord Benefield. Logos urged Tamara to learn to read also. Although hesitant at first, she learned quickly, and found it interesting to read Lady Benefield's journals, although history and philosophy bored her. Like Logos, she was surprised that sylvans hadn't invented reading. However, they both agreed that books would be hard to maintain in their wind-swept, often damp huts at New Solari.

The activity Tamara loved most was gardening with Lady Benefield in the glass house. Planting seeds, watching the seedlings come up and grow, all this was new and fascinating. She wanted to study the field crops up close, but going outside was too dangerous. When Lady Benefield began having trouble climbing up and down the stairs to the roof, Tamara took over care of the plants, following Lady Benefield's explicit instructions.

One day, rummaging through her carrying pouch for a handkerchief, Tamara found a silkiron cone, leftover from one of her forays onto the forest floor at New Solari. She took it to Lady Benefield and asked, "Do you think these seeds would germinate?"

Lady Benefield took the cone and studied it. "What kind of tree is this from?" she asked. "I don't recognize it."

"It's from a silkiron tree."

"Silkiron?"

"The tall trees we live in at New Solari."

Prying off the scales, Lady Benefield exposed the thin, overlapping seeds, the white fluff, and the single piece of gold at the core. She ran her finger over the silky thread. "Is this what the gold in your headband is made of?"

"Yes, it is."

"It must take many cones."

"Yes, we collect and save every last one we can find. Sylvans are rewarded threads for special service or because of their leadership positions, and we pass them down through our families. No strand is ever thrown away."

Lady Benefield held up one of the translucent seeds to the light. It cast a dancing miniature rainbow onto the wall. "Where do these trees grow?"

Tamara looked down. Sylvans were forbidden to give away the location of the colonies. Finally, she said, "They grow in the deep woods near the ocean."

"I mean, what kind of soil do they grow in?"

"I honestly don't know, but the ground is spongy and covered with moss."

"Then they'll need a soil that holds moisture."

Lady Benefield told Tamara how to prepare the proper soil mixture. Tamara mixed the dirt, packed it into clay pots and carried them back to her. "*You* plant the seeds," Tamara told her, "You have such good luck with plants, and I have to be sure these grow, since they're the only ones I have. I can't get any more."

Tamara watched as Lady Benefield poked holes in the soil with her knitting needle, pushed in the seeds and covered them with soil. "How long before they come up?"

Lady Benefield laughed. "You're just like the twins—so impatient."

"Am I impatient?" Tamara asked in surprise.

"Yes," Lady Benefield said, smiling.

Tamara was disconcerted. Impatience was a childish trait—seen only in young sylvans. It was also a trait of humans and, of course, the fallen.

"If the seeds dry out, they'll die," Lady Benefield said, pulling Tamara out of her trance. "I'll keep them here on my windowsill, so I'll remember to water them."

"You'll tell me as soon as they come up, won't you?" Tamara asked.

Lady Benefield smiled at her eagerness. "You'll be the first to know."

Tamara glanced at the windowsill every time she walked into the room and restrained herself from walking over to look into the pot. One morning, about three weeks later, when she entered, Lady Benefield was holding something behind her back. She pulled her arms out from behind her back and held two clay pots out to Tamara. A single sprig of neat green needles sat in the middle of each pot.

"They're up!" Tamara exclaimed. "How wonderful! Where are we going to plant them?"

"Not so fast. Pine seedlings are fragile. They need time to develop their roots before they can be transplanted. You'll find the perfect place for them, I'm sure."

***

The crowds at the front gate had thinned out while Logos was away, but when word got out that he was back and that another "angel" had arrived, people flocked to the manor house again and camped outside the gate. According to Smitty, rumors of miracles were rampant, and hundreds of people made a pilgrimage to Benefield Manor hoping to touch one of the famous 'Benefield Angels.' Lord Benefield hired two extra men and posted them at the gate with strict orders not to let anyone through without his consent.

Despite the increased security, one ingenious youth smuggled himself in underneath a wagon, and boldly walked into the kitchen whistling a tune. Rosie, not recognizing him, ran and got Smitty, who grabbed the man by his shirt and escorted him out, warning him if they caught him anywhere near the manor again, he'd be arrested. After that incident, Lord Benefield ordered the underside of all delivery carts inspected before they left the gate.

***

Soon, it wasn't only strangers who wanted in. Friends and relatives the Benefields hadn't seen for years wrote letters asking when they could come for a visit.

"Harold, I can't believe this," Lady Benefield said to her husband, waving a handful of letters in the air. "These are all from people who want to come here. You know they don't want to see *us*, they want to see the sylvans. I don't mind showing off Gabe, but I can't put Logos and Tamara on display like some side-show freaks." She dropped the letters down in front of him. "I've never seen some of these names before. Are any of these *your* relatives?"

Lord Benefield broke the wax seal and opened the first letter, pursing his lips and stroking his beard. "Hmm," he

172

said, frowning as he read through it. "This is from Edward Drew, a cousin on my mother's side. I never liked him when we were young, and I don't want to see him now." He tore it up, then opened and read a second letter and smiled. "This one is from my second cousin, Charles Benefield. I wouldn't mind seeing him again. They were at our wedding. You liked his wife, Henriette, remember?"

Lady Benefield nodded. "Oh, yes. I remember her."

Lord Benefield glanced through all the letters, sorting them into two piles, and handed her back a thin stack. "You can invite these people to come, but don't you think we'd better ask Logos and Tamara if it's all right with them?"

"You're absolutely right, I don't think Logos will have a problem, but Tamara is so shy. I'll ask Logos tonight."

As she predicted, Logos was quite open to having visitors. "That's a nice idea," he said. "I'd love to meet your friends and relatives."

"And Tamara?" Lady Benefield asked. "Do you think she'll approve? I won't have anybody here if it makes her uncomfortable."

"I'll talk to her."

As Lady Benefield predicted, Tamara wasn't thrilled with the idea. "Do I have to meet them?" she asked.

"Not if you don't want to, but you like all the humans you've met so far, don't you?"

"Yes, but I know them."

"I'm sure you'll like these people, too."

"You're probably right, but strangers make me nervous."

"I don't think it's right for us to disrupt the Benefields' social life. We've already inconvenienced them so much."

"You're right. I'm being selfish."

"Tamara said it's all right," Logos told Lady Benefield.

"Very well then. I'll invite them."

After the invitations had gone out, a steady stream of visitors began to arrive. At dinner, Tamara was quiet and reserved, speaking only when spoken to, but Logos delighted in asking questions about the visitors' lives. After dinner, Tamara excused herself and went to her room, but Logos stayed to converse with the men late into the night.

Both Logos and Tamara remained tight-lipped about sylvan life. Despite the fact that they'd both broken The Great Command—Logos by accident and Tamara on purpose—both steadfastly refused to eat anything containing meat or even meat broth.

"Logos and Tamara don't eat meat, and I don't want to offend them," Lady Benefield quietly explained to her startled guests who came expecting a feast and were served simple peasant fare: vegetables, fruit and bread, all washed down with wine.

When people asked why they didn't eat meat, Logos explained that sylvans lived on sunshine, supplemented with fruits and vegetables. He never mentioned The Great Command, or The Fall, not wanting to bring up the subject of malvans.

Once, Lady Benefield told her husband with a twinkle in her eye, "I'm starting to like this diet. Not only does it hold down expenses, but it also keeps our relatives from staying too long!"

Despite increased security, pilgrims kept climbing over the wall. They were unceremoniously thrown out. One day, a man somehow scaled the wall without being seen, got into the house by breaking a window, and followed the noise upstairs to the nursery. He ran in the room, snatched up Gabe, who was playing in a beam of sunlight on the rug, and fled down the stairs with him. Tamara and the children's screams brought the whole household running. Lord Benefield's men chased the kidnapper, and caught him before he could make it back across the wall. Gabe, who seemed to think it was a new game, was unharmed. After the man was arrested, the sheriff discovered that he was one of Lord Huntley's servants. Huntley was questioned, but swore he knew nothing about the incident.

Lord Benefield apologized to Logos and Tamara, but Logos said, "It wasn't your fault. You've done everything possible to keep us safe."

"Evidently, it wasn't enough," Lord Benefield replied, his voice bitter. "I've posted a man on each floor. No one will ever get near you again."

When they were alone in their room, Logos told a frightened Tamara. "I hate to say this, but we have to leave Benefield Manor. You or Gabe could have been kidnapped and sold—or even killed."

Tamara, unable to stop crying, nodded and hugged Gabe closer.

"I know now that we'll never be completely safe here," Logos said. "Humans will stop at nothing to reach us. They'll even break into someone's house! The Benefields have been wonderful to us, but we're putting them to great expense, and the intruders are a danger to them and their children. We need to leave—and the sooner the better."

"But where? There isn't anyplace else to go to. You said so yourself." Tamara's lips trembled, and her voice was shaky.

"Let me think about it. There must be somewhere— maybe up north."

Tamara shook her head. "Everyone knows that the tall trees don't grow where the weather is cold. We'd be forced to live on the ground, like humans—or underground like malvans." She paused and said, "Maybe that's the answer. Maybe we should move in with the malvans."

"We can't. They'd take us in, but they're monitored by the new mediator—whoever that is now—so we'd be discovered."

"Then what are we going to do?" Tamara's voice rose and became shrill.

"I don't think we have any choice but to live up north. The guards almost never fly that far, and, we can camouflage our shelter so it's not visible from the air. Maybe we'll find a habitable cave there. Give me some time to think about it. I want to study Lord Benefield's atlas first."

From then on, Tamara wouldn't let Gabe out of her sight. She moved his crib into their bedroom, double checked the locks on the window every night, but she still didn't sleep well. Even though their room was on the second floor, Logos slept with the fireplace poker next to his pillow. When his inner voice said, "*A sylvan does not resort to violence*," he silenced the thought. He knew he would protect his wife and child at any cost.

Logos and Tamara quietly made plans to leave. Chief among their concerns was how to get away without the sylvan guards seeing them. Try as they might, the only solution they could come up with was to leave next year on Blessing Day when the guards were at Flat Top Mountain, as Tamara had successfully done. Once they made up their mind, they went to the Benefields and broke the news. Lady Benefield dropped her knitting. Lord Benefield threw up his hands. "Leave? Why?"

Logos said, "We're putting everybody at risk—to say nothing of the extra expense."

"Hang the expense!" Lord Benefield shouted, pounding his fist on the table. "Where do you think you're going to go?"

"We're going to try to find an isolated spot in the far north."

"Please, don't leave," Lady Benefield begged. "You're part of our family now."

"We don't want to leave, but we think it would be best for all of us," Logos explained gently.

The Benefields kept arguing, but Logos remained firm.

***

One day when he was in the library looking through Lord Benefield's atlas again, Logos slammed the book shut and rushed off to find Tamara. He found her in the glass house watering the plants.

"What happened?" she asked, seeing the excitement on his face.

"I've thought of another place we could live. It would be safe from the guards."

Tamara set down her watering can. "Where?" she asked, her eyes searching his.

"The western lands, across the ocean. The problem is, they're so far away. I'm not sure we can fly that far."

"Are there any humans there?"

"I don't know for sure, but I don't think so."

"Tomos said his teacher claimed he found the Goddess' Grove there," Tamara said.

"Really? I've always thought that was a myth."

"Not according to his teacher. He said it's on the far west coast, and the silkiron trees are twice as tall as our trees. Tomos thought the teacher was getting senile."

"What was the teacher's name?"

"Senesses."

"Senesses! He's one of the ancients who live only on sunshine. Even he doesn't know how old he is. He's famous for his clearness of thinking. He's definitely not senile. Maybe the Goddess' Grove *does* exist."

Tamara's eyes were shining. "Let's go find it."

"Not so fast. You're forgetting how far away it is. I don't think I could make it, and I'm sure *you* couldn't."

"I could if I built up my muscles," Tamara said, flexing her arm to make a muscle.

Logos pinched her slender arm and grinned. "You call that a muscle?"

Tamara put her hands on her hips. "I'm stronger than I look, and I'm a lot lighter than you are. I bet I could make it if I built up my endurance — but I can't, because we can't fly now."

"There *is* a place we can fly," Logos said, tapping his fingers on the table. "I should have thought of it before."

"Where?"

"The horse barn. You haven't been there yet. It's a huge room with a high vaulted ceiling. There is no reason we can't exercise there—with Lord Benefield's permission, of course."

"Let's go ask him," Tamara said.

Lord Benefield said yes, but since the barn sat some distance away from the house, he insisted on Smitty escorting them over to it. Tamara exclaimed at it's great size. "This is perfect," she said. She flew for only a short time before she tired and was forced to land. She set her jaw in determination. "I'll try again tomorrow. I'll fly longer every day until I can fly non-stop like Tomos."

"Like Tomos?" Logos scoffed. "Nobody can stay aloft as long as Tomos. He holds the record."

"Then I'll work until I can fly as far as you can, and we'll hope it's enough."

Logos hugged her. "I admire your spirit. Wasn't it fun to fly again?"

"Yes, but flying indoors just isn't the same."

After a few weeks of practice, Tamara was able to double her time, but try as hard as she might, she could never fly as long as Logos could. She was always forced to land to catch her breath and rest her burning muscles.

"No use beating your wings against the wall," Logos told her. "Your time's not going to improve."

"Why not?" she asked, stomping her foot in frustration.

"You can only increase your muscles so much. You must've reached your limit."

"But Tomos can fly forever without stopping."

"The guards are selected for their large wings and strong muscles, and they train from an early age. Tomos has won the endurance championship for five years straight. You and I couldn't do what he does no matter how long we trained."

Tamara snapped her wings shut. "We can't just give up."

"Maybe I should build a boat, like the carpenter suggested," Logos said. "Then we could take Gilkenney with us."

Tamara rolled her eyes. "Don't joke. There has to be a way and I'm going to find it."

23

INVENTION

From their upstairs window, Tamara and Logos watched as Beeks' children darted around the courtyard holding an inflated pig's bladder at arms length, playing keep-away with Penny and Helen.

Logos smiled. "It's a good thing that ball doesn't float like sky pods do."

"Yes, it would get away from them, and float up in the sky out of their reach."

Suddenly, her face lit up. She turned and grabbed Logos' arms. "Logos, that's it! I could use sky pods to help me fly longer."

Logos snorted. "Sky pods are way too small. They wouldn't provide enough lift, and the air would run out of them too soon. It's a good idea, but it won't work"

"Maybe we could find a way to keep inflating them. Let's make some," she said, her eyes dancing with excitement. "I've got to try it."

"Well…"

"It might work. We won't know until we try. What do we have to lose?"

Logos threw up his hands. "All right. But what'll we make them out of?"

Tamara's smile faded. "You're right. I need silkiron fibers to make fabric, and we don't have any pods. We sure can't go back to New Solari to gather them."

Logos reached behind his head, untied his golden headband, pulled it off and handed it to her. "Here. I don't need this. You can have it."

Tamara kissed him. "That's a great idea! She pulled her headband out of her carrying pouch. "I'll use mine for the second pod. I'm going down right now and ask Lady Benefield for help."

"Why? She doesn't know anything about sky pods. She's never even seen them."

"No, but she knows how to sew. I know how to spin and weave, but I've never made pods. I need help."

***

"I need to make something," Tamara told Lady Benefield. "It will look like an inflated pigs-bladder ball, except that it's made out of four curved pieces, and the edges are overlapped to hide the seams and help keep the air in. "

"A ball made of four pieces? I've never seen anything quite like that. Can you sketch it for me?"

Tamara did her best. They cut up an old sheet and experimented until they got the shape right. Using the scraps for patterns, they pinned them on Logos and Tamara's head bands, cut them out, and sewed them together, making two almost perfectly round balls, leaving a tube at one end to blow air in.

"What are you going to do with these?" Lady Benefield asked. "Are they toys for Gabe?"

"I can't tell you just yet—it's an experiment. Thanks for helping me."

Tamara ran to show them to Logos. "Finished," she said, holding out the sky pods to Logos proudly. "What do you think?"

Logos looked doubtful. "They're way too small, but they look good. I hope they hold air."

"Let's inflate them right away. I can't wait to try them."

"How are you going to tie them to your arms?"

Tamara frowned in thought. "I could sew them to my tunic, but I think it would be better if I had some sort of harness, so I can take them off."

Tamara removed the silkiron cord from around her waist and after much trial and error, looped and knotted it around her shoulders to make a tight-fitting harness. Logos took a deep breath and inflated the pods. He squeezed hard on one. "It's holding air so far."

"Good. Let's go to the barn and try them out."

Logos asked for an escort. Smitty went with them and sat down inside the door to watch. Logos tied the pods to Tamara's harness, and they flew around and around the huge room. Smitty got to his feet a little unsteady. "You two are making me dizzy. I'll come back for you later."

"Call us when dinner is ready," Tamara shouted down to him. They flew on without stopping until Smitty reappeared and they had to descend.

"You did great!" Logos said.

"That wasn't a very long test," Tamara told Logos. "Tomorrow, I'll come out early and find out how long I can fly with them."

***

The next day, despite her best efforts, the best Tamara could manage was midafternoon. "That's still not good enough," she said.

Seeing her crestfallen face, Logos said, "You're actually doing quite well—for a sylvana."

Tamara glared at him. "Well, I didn't get to go to flying school like you did."

Logos grimaced. "I'm sorry. I meant that as a compliment."

"Apology accepted. What if I made the flotation devices bigger—not just a little bigger, but a lot bigger?"

Logos rubbed his chin. "That should work. Theoretically, the larger the pod, the greater the lift, but where would we get more material? We've already agreed we don't dare go back to collect more pods."

"You're right," Tamara said. "Let me think." She chewed on her thumbnail, her brow furrowed in deep concentration, and then her eyes lit up. "Of course! Why didn't I think of it before? I'll use my ceremonial cloak. It's huge."

"Cut up your beautiful cloak!" Logos said, his eyes wide. "Aren't you afraid lightning will strike you?"

Tamara grinned and stepped to one side. "I'm more afraid of what my mother would say if she found out, but seriously —I'm not going to need it anymore, am I?"

"No, I guess not, but still …"

"It's perfect," Tamara insisted. "I'll use it."

***

Tamara went to Lady Benefield with her cloak and told her what she needed. Tamara still hadn't said the words: sky pods, so she was startled when Lady Benefield said, "Let's make the sky pods oval, instead of round, so they won't bump into your head."

"You knew what they were all along!" Tamara exclaimed.

Lady Benefield chuckled. "Logos told us about sky pods, so I guessed. Besides, you can't keep secrets here. Smitty told me what you've been doing. Aren't you going to tell me why you need giant sky pods—and why you're willing to destroy this beautiful cloak?"

"Not yet. Maybe later, if everything works out."

Tamara's cloak had been cut out of a full circle of fabric. With Lady Benefield's skill, all they had left over when the pods were completed were a few scraps. Tamara gathered them up and put them in her carrying pouch.

Tamara and Logos carried the pods to the barn before inflating them. Gilkenney followed them in, but made a nuisance of himself pouncing on the ties and had to be set outside. The pods took a long time to inflate. Logos got winded and had to stop and rest several times. When Smitty volunteered to help, Logos thanked him but gently explained that only sylvan breath would work.

At maximum size, the pods were almost as tall as Tamara. They had a lot of lift, too, and when Logos tied them to her harness, he had to hold onto her to keep her on the ground. Finally, he released her for her test flight. She floated straight up and bumped into the ceiling. Laughing, Logos flew up and pulled her down.

"Now there's *too* much lift," she said, pouting.

"You need to change the angle of your wing strokes—like this—watch." He demonstrated the flying technique he had been taught in flight school.

Tamara practiced the strokes, and tried again. It worked, and she was able to fly without stopping. When Smitty came back at dinnertime, she said, "I'm not tired at all. I'm going to keep flying. Tell the Benefields not to order any extra peas for dinner."

After dinner, Smitty came back. Except for an undetermined amount of time when she fell asleep and Logos let her sleep, floating against the ceiling, Tamara flew all night. She probably would have flown non-stop the next day, if Logos hadn't made her stop. "We'll need energy for the trip," he said the next morning. "Let's go to the glass house and sun."

Tamara descended. "They work. We'll be able to make it," she said as Logos worked to free the pods from her shoulders.

"Yes, I'm so proud of you." Logos untied the cords which tied off the pods and released them. The pods spiraled crazily around the room and one of them hit Smitty, making them laugh. Logos retrieved the pods and then they fetched Gabe and went to the glass house to sun. Rolling out mats, they lay down on the floor and stretched out their wings. Gabe rolled onto his stomach and twitched his miniature wings in the sunshine.

"This is my favorite place," Tamara said. "I love being surrounded by living things, and the fresh air they put out is wonderfully bracing, but the sunlight isn't quite right. Something's missing. Haven't you noticed?"

"Yes. No matter how long I sun, I'm always a little hungry. I don't know if it's because the light is filtered, or if it has something to do with being fallen."

Tamara rested her head on her elbows. "Do you think being fallen affects how we absorb sunshine?"

"I've never heard that, but most of the fallen resort to eating meat. Maybe it's because they're hungry all the time."

"I'll never eat meat again," Tamara declared.

"Nor I."

"We'll have to take pea seeds with us," Tamara said chuckling.

***

When the pair showed up for dinner with glowing cheeks and shining eyes, Lord Benefield said. "You two have been hiding out in the barn for days. Don't you think it's about time you told us what you're up to?"

Tamara and Logos exchanged glances. "We've found a place to live," Logos said.

"Where?" Lord and Lady Benefield said in unison.

"Remember when I told you that a large land mass exists across the ocean?" Logos asked.

Lord Benefield nodded.

"That's where we're going."

Lord Benefield stared open mouthed. "But, it's too far to cross."

"We think we can make it," Logos said. He turned to Lady Benefield. "The sky pods you made are giving Tamara the extra lift she needs to fly long distances."

"So that's what you need them for!" Lady Benefield said to Tamara. "Now I wish I hadn't made them. When are you leaving?"

"Tonight," Logos said. "Before you talk us out of it."

24

BEGINNINGS

"Not tonight!" Lady Benefield exclaimed."

We apologize for the short notice," Logos said, "but we don't know what the weather will be like there, and we're anxious to get there and get settled. Since we'll have to fly both day and night, a full moon is a necessity, and the moon is almost full now. We're leaving now as soon as it's dark. We think we have a better chance of escaping the guard that way. They wouldn't expect us to fly that late at night."

Lady Benefield's eyes teared up. "You won't be here to see my new baby." She cupped her huge abdomen. "—or babies."

"Don't upset yourself, Mary," Lord Benefield said, patting his wife's arm. "We both knew they would leave eventually."

"But not this soon! What'll I tell the children?"

"Logos and I will break the news to them ourselves," Tamara said.

After an early dinner, Logos and Tamara went to the twins' room and told them that they were leaving. The girls flung themselves at Tamara, clung to her, cried and begged her not to go. Tamara dried their tears and explained—without mentioning the kidnapping—why they had to leave. She told them how unsafe they felt every time they stepped out of the house—how much they missed not being able to fly outdoors. The girls listened with sober faces and soon calmed down. "In that case, we have presents for you," Penny said. "We were going to give them to you for Christmas, but since you're leaving, we'll give them to you now." The two of them dived into their sewing baskets.

"This is for Gabe." Proudly, Helen held out her gift: knitted wing covers with a drawstring to hold them on. "Mother spun the yarn," Helen said. "I helped comb the wool myself."

Penny had made tiny booties. Tamara took the presents. "Thank you. They're beautiful, and they're light enough to take with us." Her glance at Logos dared him to say no. "I'll keep them, and after Gabe grows up I'll show them to him and tell him about the two wonderful little girls who made them."

Tamara managed to maintain her composure until she and Logos returned to their room where she broke down sobbing. "I'll never see them again — the twins — the Benefields — my mother and father — New Solari!"

Logos pulled her close to him. "We can still stay here," he said, brushing off her tears with his thumbs. "We'll manage somehow."

"No, no. We must leave. I know that. I'm just being silly. It's only that the finality of it all just hit me. I'll be all right."

Someone knocked at the door. Logos opened it to find the Benefields who had brought gifts, too. Lady Benefield waddled in, rubbing her back. She gave Logos a cloth sling she had made out of the scraps of Tamara's cape. She said, "I thought it would allow you to carry Gabe close to your body and leave your hands free."

"Thanks! That's a great idea!" Logos exclaimed.

For Tamara, she had a small pair of scissors. "They're the smallest, lightest scissors I own, and they're sharp. I thought you might need them in your new home."

Tamara hugged her. "Thank you. We won't have any tools where we're going, so they'll be very useful. I'll think of you every time I use them."

"Logos. I want you to have this to remember me by," Lord Benefield said. He handed Logos a small, hollow-handled knife, the blade of which was flat on one side and convex on the other.

"But, this is your quill knife for cutting quill pens!" Logos exclaimed.

"Yes. I'd love to send along some books, but I know they're too heavy. You'll have to write your own books."

"Me?" Logos asked.

"You and Tamara. You're the only sylvans who can read and write. Someone needs to preserve the history of your civilization. Who better than you two?"

"What would we use for paper and ink?" Logos asked.

"You can make paper yourself."

"How?" Logos asked.

"You pound plants into a pulp and spread it out in thin sheets to dry. He winked at Tamara. Of course, someone would need to experiment to find the right plants."

Tamara's eyes were shining.

"What about ink?" Logos asked.

"Hmm," Benefield said. "You can dissolving ashes in water or juice."

"I know of several berries that stain things permanently," Tamara said. "Walnut hulls do too. We'll find something to make ink out of."

You'll need to make pens, too," Lord Benefield said. "I think you know where to find feathers."

Everyone laughed. Lady Benefield caught her breath and rubbed her back again.

"Is anything wrong?" Tamara asked. "You aren't going into labor are you?"

"No—no. I'm not due for another week. I must have twisted my back—oh!" she exclaimed and sat down on a chair.

"You're tired, Mary," her husband said. "Why don't you lie down for a while and have Lizzie give you a nice back rub?"

"All right," Lady Benefield said, "but I'll be there to say goodbye, even if Harold has to carry me up the stairs."

Logos and Tamara glanced at each other nervously.

"What?" the Benefields asked.

"We don't want to be rude, but we think it would be better to say our good-byes inside. A crowd on the roof might attract attention from the guards. We'll leave from our balcony. Why don't you come to our room instead?"

"I'll be there," Lady Benefield said.

"Me, too," Lord Benefield said, ushering his wife out.

"As soon as they closed the door," Logos said, "Let's take a nap, too. We'll need all the energy we can get tomorrow."

***

Logos and Tamara had just got to sleep when someone knocked on their door.

"Who is it?" Logos called out.

"It's me, Lizzie."

Logos opened the door to find a white faced Lizzie. "It's Lady Benefield," she said, her voice full of concern. "It seems the back pain she's been experiencing all day wasn't just a muscle strain. She's in labor. Lord Benefield sent for the midwife, but Lady Benefield is asking for Tamara."

Tamara and Logos rushed to Lady Benefield's room. They found her in bed, rolling from side to side in pain. A contraction hit, and she gasped and doubled over. "Tamara, help me!" she pleaded.

Pulling Logos aside, Tamara whispered in a frantic voice, "I don't know what to do. I've never witnessed a birth."

"Don't worry," Logos said. "I'm sure the midwife will be here soon. Just make her as comfortable as you can."

Tamara adjusted Lady Benefield's pillows, held her hand, and fanned her with her wings. Lord Benefield paced around the room wiping the sweat off his brow.

"Sit down, Harold," his wife ordered. "You're making me nervous." He sat down, but a few moments later, he jumped up, looked out the door for Smitty and started pacing again. Logos tried unsuccessfully to distract him with conversation.

Between contractions, Lady Benefield kept insisting everything was fine, but her voice grew weaker.

Smitty ran in, his face creased with worry. "The midwife is out delivering another baby. I left word for her to come here immediately when she gets home."

Lord Benefield smashed his fist on the door. "This is all my fault. I should have hired a midwife to live here. What'll we do now?"

Tamara darted a questioning look at Logos, and Logos realized he couldn't keep his connection with Huntley Manor a secret any longer. "I know a midwife," he said.

Lord Benefield looked at him in amazement. "You do?" he asked. "Who?"

"Neela Pratt. She's a servant at Huntley Manor."

Benefield stroked his beard. "Yes. I remember her now. He looked at his wife. "Wasn't she Leutha Huntley's governess?"

Lady Benefield gave a faint nod and mumbled something unintelligible.

"How do you know about her?" Benefield asked.

When Logos didn't reply, Benefield said, "Never mind I didn't mean to pry. I didn't think Neela was still alive. She must be as old as Methuselah. Yes, she was a midwife." He turned to Smitty. "Have a carriage brought around immediately. Go to Huntley Manor and fetch Neela Pratt here as fast as possible."

"Yes, Mi'Lord!" Smitty said as he ran out the door.

Logos said, "I can't just sit here and wait. I'll fly over to Huntley Manor and notify Neela, so she'll be ready to go when Smitty arrives."

Tamara's eyes widened, and Lord Benefield said, "No. That's too dangerous! You could be caught."

But Logos was already out in the hall. "I'll be careful," he called back. Running out the front door, he jumped into flight with a *whoosh*. The warm, sweet air rushed up to support him. He flew around the stables to avoid the crowd by the gate. Then he flew low to the ground until he got out of sight of the house. He didn't know exactly where Huntley Manor was, but he knew where both Huntley Manor and Benefield Manor were in relation to New Solari, so he should be able to calculate a bearing. His rings didn't seem to be working, so he took his position from the sun. He flew low to the trees and kept a sharp ear out for guards.

He had forgotten how good the cool air felt under his wings. He stopped himself from whistling.

The farther he got from Benefield Manor, the more relaxed and confident he became. Before long, he saw a clearing and saw Huntley Manor's outlying fields and recognized the large house. He flew down and landed on Neela's balcony and tapped on the door.

Neela threw open the door. "I wasn't expectin' you, Lord Logos, but you're always welcome here. I figured you must be one of those 'Benefield angels everyone's talkin' about. What are you doin' here? I thought you weren't finding homes for babies anymore."

"I'm not."

"How can I help you then?"

"We need you at Benefield Manor. Lady Benefield is having a baby and she's in trouble. Her midwife isn't available. Will you come?"

"Of course. I'll get dressed and ask for a wagon right away."

"No need. Lord Benefield has sent his wife's carriage for you."

Neela chuckled. "Fancy that—me in a grand lady's carriage!"

Someone rapped on her hallway door. Neela jumped and then cracked open the door. Lady Huntley, holding Leuthur in her arms, pushed her way into the room. "Sorry to bother you, but Leuthur's running a little fever — oh!" she exclaimed as she caught sight of Logos.

Logos stared in open-mouthed amazement at Leuthur.

"He came to tell me they need me at Benefield Manor," Neela said.

"What's wrong?" Lady Huntley asked. "Is Mary all right? Is she due yet?"

"The baby is comin', and she's in trouble. They're sending over a carriage for me."

"That won't be necessary," Lady Huntley said. She went to the door and spoke to a servant in the hall. "Order my carriage brought around immediately. Tell the driver to take Neela to Benefield Manor." Turning back to Neela, she said, "Tell my cousin I'm praying for her, and when you get home, come and tell me how she is." She cast an appraising look at Logos.

"I will, Mi'Lady," Neela said.

As soon as Neela closed the door, Logos spun her around. "That's the baby boy I dropped off here, isn't it? The night I had my accident."

"Shh!" Neela hissed. "Yes, it is. I'll explain on the way over. Turn around so's I can get dressed."

Neela threw on her clothes and plodded downstairs behind an impatient Logos. When Lady Huntley's carriage pulled up, the driver jumped down to assist Neela. He saw Logos and stopped short.

"Whatcha lookin' at?" Neela snapped. "Let's go."

Keeping a watchful eye on Logos, the man helped Neela up the steps into Lady Huntley's elegant silk-lined carriage. Soft wool blankets were stacked on the seats.

Neela unfolded one and spread it across her lap. Logos took the seat opposite her, and the driver closed the door. "Now tell me what's going on," Logos demanded. "Why is that baby still here?"

Neela sighed. "Lord Huntley made me swear not to breathe a word to anyone, but being as you already know, I might as well explain. His own son died that night after you left, and he switched the babies."

Logos groaned and steepled his hands across his mouth. "Oh, Goddess! Does Lady Huntley know?"

"No — and she can't find out." Neela burst out. "She worships that child."

"Does Lord Huntley know that I brought the baby?"

"No. He thinks Leuthur is a villager's son. I never told him you brung him."

Logos wiped a shaking hand across his brow. Lord Huntley, the sworn enemy of malvans. What would happen if Huntley found out the child he was raising as his own son and heir was malvan-born? "Does he love the boy?" Logos asked.

Neela took her time replying. "I don't think so. He don't pay the child no never mind, and he gets angry and leaves the room whenever he cries. I know this sounds awful, but he acts jealous."

"He must never find out where the boy came from. I can't tell you why. You'll just have to trust me. Promise me you won't tell him."

"Of course I won't," Neela said, drawing herself up into a huff. "I'm keepin' Lord Huntley's secret, and I'll keep yours." She leaned forward. "Lady Huntley is bound to ask what you was doin' in my room and how you knew I'm a midwife. What'll I tell her?"

Logos thought for a few seconds. "Tell her that Lady Benefield remembered you and sent me to fetch you."

Neela crinkled up her already wrinkled face. "What'll I tell her when she asks how you knew where my room was?"

Logos thought for a moment. "Tell her you went out on your balcony for a breath of fresh air and I saw you."

Neela leaned back in the seat and looked more content. The driver galloped the horses as hard as he dared, and about halfway to Benefield Manor, they met the Benefield carriage charging its way to Huntley Manor. Logos hailed the driver and told him to turn around and go back.

***

An anxious Lord Benefield came out to meet the carriage. "Thank you for coming at such short notice, Miss Pratt," he said as he helped her down.

She curtsied. "I'm just plain Neela. Take me to Lady Mary."

Benefield escorted her to his wife's bedroom. Neela stopped at the door. "You men make yourselves useful and bring me some sheets and a pail of hot water."

She entered the room and stopped short when she saw Tamara. "Who are you?" she asked and then immediately said, "I know. You must be Logos' sweetheart."

"Yes," Tamara said, "but we're married now."

After she examined the woman, Neela told Lord Benefield, "Good thing Lord Logos came for me. She has two of 'em and they're all jumbled up.

Lord Benefield and Logos opened the door and walked in, Benefield lugging a pail of hot water, Logos carrying a stack of sheets and blankets.

"Just set 'em down," Neela snapped. "Now get back outside and don't come in 'til I tell you." The two of them looked at each other, turned and left.

Neela turned her attention to her patient. As the twins were born, Neela handed the babies to Tamara who wrapped them in blankets and tucked them in on either side of Lady Benefield.

Outside the door, Lord Benefield heard the babies crying and stuck his head in the door. "May I come in now?" he asked, sounding like a schoolboy.

"Yes. Come in, Harold," Lady Mary called. "You, too, Logos."

They entered and walked to her side. "We have another set of twins." Lady Benefield told her husband.

"That's wonderful," he said. He turned to Neela. "Are they going to be all right?"

"Everyone's fine—Lady Benefield will be on her feet in a few days."

"I don't know how to thank you ..." Benefield said.

"You're welcome, sir," Neela said.

"You'll stay the night, won't you?" Benefield asked her. "It's almost dark."

"Yes—if'n you don't mind, I'll catch some sleep and go back in the mornin'."

"Stay as long as you like," Benefield said.

"Lizzie, show Neela to a guest room and have the bath filled with hot water," Lady Benefield told her maid.

"That would be grand," Neela said. She said goodnight and followed Lizzie out.

"I'm indebted to you, too, Logos," Benefield said. "You got Neela here a lot faster—at great personal risk, I might add."

Logos bowed.

Sitting down on the edge of the bed, Benefield pulled back the infants' blankets to look at their faces. "Do you suppose they're identical twins again?" he asked his wife.

"Definitely not," she replied.

Confusion registered across Benefield's face. "All babies look alike. How can you be so sure?"

Lady Benefield smiled. "Because one's a boy and one's a girl. You finally have a son and heir, Harold Benefield."

"That's wonderful," he said, beaming. "Which one's the boy?"

"The one on the right — I think."

"What about names?"

"What would you think about naming them after Logos and Tamara?"

"I think that's a wonderful idea!"

The sylvans looked at each other and smiled. "What an honor! Thank you!" Logos exclaimed.

"You aren't still leaving tonight, are you?" Lady Benefield asked them.

Logos hesitated and glanced at Tamara." Yes, I think we should. Apparently, there's no guard today. I didn't see any sign of guards on my way to Huntley Manor."

"I won't be able to come see you off," Lady Benefield said.

"There is no reason we can't leave from your window," Logos said.

***

The time to leave came all to soon. Logos lowered Gabe into Lady Benefield's arms. Gabe smiled and grabbed at her religious medal. "Good bye, Gabe. I wish you could stay here and grow up with the new twins," she said, kissing him and handing him back to Logos who tucked him inside his new carrying pouch.

Glancing at the windowsill, Lady Benefield said, "Tamara, don't forget your seedlings."

"May I take them?" Tamara asked Logos.

Logos shook his head. "I'm sorry. They're far too heavy. Besides, I'm sure we'll find tall trees in our new home."

Tamara's face fell. Lady Benefield said, "If you take them out of their pots, they won't weigh much at all."

Tamara looked at Logos. "What if we don't find the grove? What if there aren't any silkiron trees across the ocean?"

"All right," Logos said, "I know when I'm out-argued. You can take them."

Tamara thanked him with a brilliant smile, slid the tiny plants out of the pots, rolled them in silkiron scraps and laid them gently in the bottom of her carrying pouch. "A part of New Solari to take with me," she said. She kissed the newborns and gave Lady Benefield a long hug. "Good-bye. You've been like a mother to me. I'll never forget you."

"Nor I you, daughter," Lady Benefield replied, her voice choking up.

At that, the twins sobbed, clutched Tamara, and had to be pulled away. Logos pushed open the balcony door. Lord Benefield stepped forward and clasped Logos' shoulders. "Remember—if this doesn't work out, you're always welcome to come back."

"Thank you, sir—and thank you for everything you've done for us."

"Let's give the humans a thrill," Logos said. He jumped into the air and flew straight at the gate. Tamara followed close behind, and the milling crowd screamed and ducked as the sylvans passed right over their heads.

***

Logos and Tamara flew straight for the coast at maximum speed. This was the most critical part of their trip. Once over the ocean, they would be less likely to be noticed by any stray guards. Logos had Tamara's deflated sky pods wrapped around his waist. Since she could fly faster without the sky pods, they had decided to wait to inflate them until after they reached the coast.

The Goddess was just starting into the sixth arc. They sped on in silence, making excellent time and enjoying the fresh air. The coastline was in sight, and they had begun their descent when they heard powerful wings drubbing the air behind them. A deep voice shouted, "Stop!"

25

TOMOS' DECISION

Tamara turned, saw Tomos and screamed, "Tomos, no!"

Ignoring her, Tomos seized Logos by his long wing bones and snapped his wings shut, stopping Logos in midair. The extra weight caused Tomos to drop perilously close to the ground. He skimmed briefly over the marsh, then adjusted his flight pattern, gained altitude and headed straight for New Solari. Tamara followed, screaming at Tomos to stop. Logos twisted his head to shout at Tomos: "Can't we go down and talk this over?"

"There's nothing to discuss," Tomos replied. "You're going back with me."

Tamara put on a burst of speed and flew in front of Tomos, forcing him to brake to avoid knocking her out of the air.

"Get out of the way, Tamara," Tomos said.

"No, I won't! Please, stop, Tomos," she pleaded, "Stop so we can talk!" She headed for the ground. Tomos released Logos with a shove and followed her, and they landed in a grassy field near the edge of the salt marsh.

Tomos jabbed his finger in Logos' chest and yelled, "What do you think you're doing—and why do you have Tamara's cloak wrapped around you?"

"We're going across the ocean to live, and this isn't her cloak," Logos replied, rolling his shoulders and rubbing his pinched wing muscles.

"Across the ocean!" Tomos exclaimed. "Are you completely insane? That sounds like something a flagit would think up."

Logos' fists clenched; Tomos put his hand on his sling. Tamara stepped between them, and Tomos let go of his sling. "Why are you leaving?" he asked. "I thought you liked those humans you've been living with."

"We do," Tamara answered. "They're like family to us, and they tried their best to protect us, but Gabe was kidnapped anyway! We were a terrible burden to them."

Blood rushed to Logos' head, and the words tumbled out of his mouth: "Yes, we almost lost Gabe—and what's more, we're tired of not being able to go outside to sun or to fly—all because of you and your flajiting guards, hounding us day and night …"

Tamara turned, caught Logos' eye and shook her head. He shut up. She was right as usual. He had to stay calm. He didn't have anything to gain from antagonizing Tomos. Their only hope was to reason with him. "I'm sorry," he said. He took a deep breath and forced his voice to stay steady. "We've found a way to cross the ocean safely. Once across, we'll never be a threat to anyone."

"He's right," Tamara said. "How could we possibly be a threat? We'll be all alone there."

"None of this matters. I took an oath to return you, and I'm honor bound to keep it," Tomos said with excessive heat.

Tamara sighed, glanced sideways at Logos and stepped closer to Tomos. "I have to tell you something."

"Tamara, don't!" Logos exclaimed.

"Nothing you can say will make any difference," Tomos said.

"This will—I'm contaminated," Tamara blurted out.

Tomos' eyes widened. "You're lying! You're just saying that to get out of going back."

Tamara flinched. "I don't lie."

"I'm sorry, Tamara. I didn't mean that," Tomos said.

"It's the truth, Tomos. I've looked in the mirror and I can see I've changed," she said. "Look at my eyes."

Tomos stepped closer to study her eyes. He turned on Logos, his jaw muscles clenching and unclenching. "You're responsible for this. You forced her to eat meat, didn't you?"

"Are you kidding? I'd never do that!"

"Logos had nothing to do with it. I did it myself," Tamara said.

"But—why?"

"It was the only way I could think of to get to stay with him."

Tomos frowned and looked down as though struggling with a decision. When he looked up again, his face was stern. "Contaminated or not, an oath is an oath. I must take you back home."

Tamara's eyes were pleading at Logos for help, and Logos didn't know what to do. Then, he had an idea—a totally unscrupulous idea. "Do you want Tamara to live on Flat-Top Mountain?" he asked in a challenging voice.

Horror flashed over Tomos' face.

"Think about it," Logos added. "What else could the Council do? They couldn't allow her to live in the colonies. Even her father couldn't manage that."

When Tomos still didn't say anything, Logos pressed on. "Imagine Tamara living with those violent sylvans—those flagits. Do you really think a few guards could protect her?"

"Stop!" Tomos snapped. "You're right. I'd never let her be taken to Flat-Top Mountain."

Logos tried not to smirk. His shot had hit home.

Tomos shouted, "None of this would have happened if you'd gone to Flat Top Mountain peacefully, instead of sneaking off like a thief in the middle of the night."

Logos grimaced. This fact was indisputable.

"Don't blame Logos," Tamara said. "He ran away to protect Gabe. He couldn't possibly have known what I intended to do—I didn't even know it myself at that point." She stepped up to Tomos and took his hands. "You once said you loved me. If you ever loved me, please let us go."

Tomos stared at her for a few moments and then gave a long sigh and dropped her hands. He turned to Logos. "All right, you win. I won't take her home—but you're not taking her across this ocean. Why can't you go somewhere else—like farther up north?"

"Because her father will never give up," Logos said. "No place on this side of the ocean is safe. He'll look for her until he finds her—you know that's true, don't you?"

Tomos sighed and nodded.

"You told me once that you wanted to fly across the ocean—that you were the only sylvan strong enough to do it." He stopped and let this thought sink in. "Listen, we can make it," Logos said. He put his hands on his waist. "Tamara made these extra-large sky pods. They allow her to fly a long distance without tiring." He unwrapped the pods from around his waist and handed one of them to Tomos.

Looking skeptical, Tomos examined the pod in the failing light.

"They work—I can show you," Tamara said.

"All right. Show me," Tomos said, handing the pod to Tamara.

Tamara puffed out her cheeks and blew into the pod. Logos started on the other one. When Tamara paused to catch her breath, Tomos took the pod from her and blew into it. As the sun sank closer to the horizon, the pods filled out into their pear shape. Logos tied them to Tamara's harness and put his hands on her shoulders. "Look," he said. "I have to hold her down to keep her from floating off."

"All right, so they have good lift, but how long will they last?" Tomos asked.

"They're basically the same as children's pods," Tamara explained. "They'll stay inflated for at least one arc, and we can add more air while we're flying."

Tomos scratched his chin. "They might do the job, but I still can't let you go."

Tamara's face fell. Logos cast about in his mind for another argument and found none. He had failed.

"I can't let you go," Tomos repeated. He paused and added: "—alone—I'm coming with you."

Tamara's smiled beamed, but it took a moment longer for Logos to understand. A look of amazement appeared on his face. "You mean we can go? Thank you …"

"Don't thank me, you idiot," Tomos snapped. "I'm not doing this for you. I'm doing it for Tamara. Let's get started before one of the fire-spotters wonders what's keeping me so long and comes to look for me."

Tomos took to the air, and Logos and Tamara followed, flying side by side at a safe distance.

Soon, they were so far out from land that all they saw was water and the setting sun. The sunset was spectacular. Low-lying clouds turned a fiery red, and the light reflected up on the higher layers, tinting them shades of pink and lavender. As the sun sank into the Goddess' bower, the full moon rose behind them, spilling a silver pathway across the surface of the water. "Oh, look!" Tamara said to Logos, "Did you ever see anything so lovely?"

Logos grunted.

"I've never flown over the ocean," Tamara said. "I never dreamed it would be so beautiful."

Logos didn't answer.

"You're still upset—aren't you?" Tamara asked.

"Yes, I am," he grumbled. "I wasn't counting on having my old rival along for company."

"He's not your rival any more," Tamara said. "Besides, don't you understand how fortunate this is for us? We have a better chance of getting across now. Tomos has full navigation rings, so we won't fly in the wrong direction and get lost."

Logos realized he hadn't thought much about navigation. He'd just assumed they'd follow the setting sun. What would they do on cloudy days? Tomos' eye rings would be an advantage. Tomos was also the strongest flyer in New Solari. They *were* lucky to have him with them.

"You're probably right," he admitted but having Tomos along still galled him. As he watched Tomos flying effortlessly in front of them, he fought down his jealousy and concentrated on copying Tomos' wing strokes.

***

The moon rose to rule the sky. Tamara kept up with Logos and Tomos for a long time, before she started to lag behind. They took her hands and towed her, allowing her to fold her wings and rest. They could only tow her for a short amount of time, though, for the drag slowed them down, and they gradually drifted closer to the sea.

Eventually, Tamara dropped their hands and flew on her own again, but she didn't fly for as far as she had before. Although he couldn't see all the pods very well by moonlight, Logos wondered if they had started to leak air. The next time Tamara tired, Tomos carried her for a long time before releasing her. Logos noted with satisfaction that Tomos held her out at a respectful distance.

At dawn, Tamara's head started nodding. Tomos and Logos noticed and flew closer to her. Several times, she caught herself and snapped her head upright. Then she fell asleep. When she awoke, Logos and Tomos were towing her by the pods. They streamed over the water, the sun casting their long shadows eerily ahead of them. Gabe was sleeping with his mouth open, making little baby snores.

"Sorry," Tamara said, "Let me go. I'm awake now." They released her and she broke into flight.

Logos fell back to talk to Tomos. "I'm getting sleepy too," Logos admitted. "What are we going to do? I don't want Tamara to try to tow me. It would tire her too much."

"Let me know when the feeling gets overwhelming. I'll carry you, so you can sleep," Tomos said.

"Are you sure you can carry me?"

"Of course. I've carried sylvans a lot heavier than you."

"What about you? When will you sleep?"

"I can fly in my sleep."

Logos could have sworn a brief grin flashed across Tomos' face.

"I'm used to staying up all night," Tomos explained. "Not to brag, but I can go for days without sleeping. In order to qualify as a long-distance flyer, you have to be able to. However, if I start to nod off, hit me. If one of us falls into the water, we might not be able to get out."

***

So they made it easily through the first full day and second night, without any major incidents, Logos and Tomos occasionally towing Tamara, and Tomos carrying Logos for short spells so he could nap.

When the second morning arrived, to Logos' delight, a brisk tailwind began to blow, pushing them forward with little effort on their part. "How far do you think we've gone?" Logos asked Tomos.

"I don't really know," Tomos replied. "I've never crossed the ocean before, but we just passed one of the major force lines. Didn't you feel the vibration?"

Embarrassed, Logos shook his head. So it was just as he feared. His internal navigation was completely gone now. He might as well be human.

Mid-morning, a school of dolphins followed them, leaping in graceful arcs over the waves and landing with little splashes. Tamara was fascinated, and Gabe shouted and laughed every time one of the dolphins jumped. In other times, Logos would have enjoyed the sight too, but he was too concerned about how much longer they had to fly. He didn't say anything to Tamara, but her pods had visibly shrunk.

Tomos saw Logos looking up at the pods and flew over to talk to him. "They need to be reinflated," Tomos said, "—now while the weather is still good."

"Are you expecting a storm? The sky is perfectly clear."

"The air is lighter," Tomos said, shooting a disdainful glance at him. "Less buoyant. Can't you feel that either?"

Logos didn't reply. They discussed the situation and decided on the best course of action. Logos flew over to tell Tamara what they intended to do. He picked her up, and Tomos joined them. Tamara removed a pod. Tomos blew into it. When Tomos got winded, they switched places, Tomos holding Tamara, and Logos blowing into the pod. When the pod was fully inflated, they tied off the end and reattached it, Tamara weaving the loose ends in and out of her harness to keep them from flapping in the breeze. They repeated the procedure with the other pod. The work tired out Logos more than he wanted to admit, but the additional loft did permit Tamara to fly alone for quite a while longer, taking some of the burden off both him and Tomos.

Mid afternoon, the tailwind, which up to now had been their friend, turned gusty, forcing them to greater heights for fear of being dashed into the sea. At the higher altitude, the pods shrank again. The high winds made it impossible to tow Tamara, so Tomos carried her more often. Tomos still seemed as strong as when they'd started. Logos was getting terribly tired.

Near sunset, the winds died down, permitting them to reinflate the pods again. They had no sooner finished and released Tamara, than the clouds thickened, covering the rising moon and leaving them in the dark. Tamara cried out, "Logos, where are you?"

"Here!" Logos yelled.

"I don't know where I am," she replied. "I'm afraid I'll get too close to the ocean." She sounded panic stricken.

Tomos yelled, "Fly towards my voice—both of you. Stay close enough to hear my wings. I can tell how far I am above the water by feeling the wind from my wings rebounding off the water."

They did as Tomos ordered, but the night got darker as the sun set, and seemed endless. Several times, Tomos shouted at them to stay fly higher. Despite Logos carrying Tamara often to let her nap, she fell asleep twice, and each time, Tomos heard her falling and grabbed her. Once, Logos awoke with a jolt when Tomos yelled at him to wake up. Tomos was carrying Tamara and dragging him by a wing. Logos broke into flight, patted Gabe's pouch, and sighed in relief when he felt his warm body.

Tomos released Tamara. He yelled at Tomos, "You're supposed to tell me when you're getting too sleepy, I almost didn't catch you!"

"I'm sorry," Logos said. "I do need a nap." Tomos was right, he had been stupid to think that they were strong enough to cross this ocean on their own. They never would've got this far without him. Thank the Goddess Tomos was with them. He folded his wings, Tomos grabbed him, he closed his eyes, slacked his muscles and he was instantly asleep.

***

Morning dawned clear, with a gentle tail wind, and they seized the opportunity to reinflate Tamara's pods. After the task was done, everyone looked strong, and all seemed well. Without warning, Tomos' head fell forward, and he dropped. Tamara screamed. Logos dove and managed to grab a wing and stop him before he hit the water. He strained his muscles to fly with all his strength. He was surprised by Tomos' weight. Tomos awoke, broke free and apologized, red-faced.

"It's all right," Logos said. "You've been awake for three days. What do you expect? Thanks to you, I'm wide awake, and Tamara's pods are in good shape. I'll spell you."

"I don't know. I'm pretty heavy."

"I know, but I'll try."

Tomos folded his wings, and Logos grasped him under his arms. Tomos fell asleep immediately. Logos adjusted his wing strokes for the additional load. Tomos weighed more than twice as much as Tamara, and carrying him was more difficult than he expected. He gritted his teeth and fought to carry Tomos' dead weight. Tamara flew up next to them. "I'll take Gabe," she said.

"It's ... too hard ... to move ... the sling," Logos grunted. "Besides ... Gabe's ... so ... light ... wouldn't ... make ... any ... difference."

His chest and wing muscles burning, Logos struggled on. *A sylvan does not admit to pain* he reminded himself every time he thought he couldn't go on. Finally, his wing muscles began to tremble, and he knew they were about to give out. He was forced to yell at Tomos and wake him. "I'm sorry, I have to let you go," he said.

"No matter," Tomos said as he resumed flight. "That helped a lot. Tamara must need a rest. I'll spell her."

"How did you fall sleep so fast?" Tamara asked when Tomos picked her up.

"I've trained myself to fall asleep almost instantly. An instructor told me the secret. It's very useful."

"Can you teach me?"

"Sure. It's all in the breathing. When you're counting breaths in and out, you can't think of anything else and the mind gets bored and gives up."

"Tell me how to count."

Tomos laughed. "As slow as you can until your chest is full, hold, and then let out as slow as you can."

"I'll try it," Tamara said, "One ... two ... three ..."

They were fortunate that Tomos had caught a nap, because as the sun climbed passed its highpoint, the crosswinds picked up, and he spent most of the afternoon spelling Logos and Tamara. Towards evening, the main air currents changed direction and came from the northeast, and cold gusts dashed them back and forth. They had to keep a greater distance apart to avoid colliding with one another. Gabe crowed in delight each time they blew sideways. Tamara tired quickly and looked exhausted. Glancing up, Logos noticed that her sky pods were shrinking rapidly. He wondered how much longer they would provide lift. Increasingly anxious, he waved Tomos over. "The pods are losing too much air," he said, "and Tamara needs them more than ever right now."

"I know. We need to reinflate them again."

"In these winds?"

"We don't have any choice. I was hoping the winds would die down—instead they've picked up. We'd better do it now, before they get any worse."

"All right," Logos said in a resigned voice, "but I'm not sure I can hang on to the pods."

"Are you strong enough to carry Tamara?"

"I think so."

"Good. You hold her. I'll reinflate the pods by myself."

Logos explained the plan to Tamara. She looked frightened, but she nodded, and Logos picked her up. She started loosening a pod. As she untied the knot, the wind jerked the pod out of her hands, and it shot up into the sky with a *whoosh*.

Tomos swore and gave chase. "Uh, oh!" Logos exclaimed as the pod started into the clouds. Tomos could easily lose the pod.

Tomos charged full speed into the cloud and disappeared. Logos' eyes remained locked on the spot where he had last seen him.

A few moments later, Tomos dropped down below the clouds, the pod trailing behind him. Logos and Tamara cheered. Tomos resumed work on the pod. Alternately, he carried the pod up high and then glided down, blowing into it. In the brisk winds, inflating the pod was slow work, but it gradually grew larger.

After the pod reached maximum size, Tomos held on to the pod while Tamara secured it. Tomos said, "Good. Now give me the other one." He shot an accusing look at Logos. "Help her hold on to the cursed thing this time."

After both pods had been inflated, Tamara flew easier. However, carrying her had further taxed Logos' strength. He was near exhaustion and for the first time, he began to wonder if he would be able to make it. "If I don't make it, you'll take care of Tamara, won't you?" he asked Tomos.

"What do you mean? We'll make it," Tomos said, then added, "Of course I'll take care of her."

That evening, the winds calmed down, but the sky turned an ugly red. Logos didn't need to feel the pressure change to know that a red sky meant bad weather, and sure enough, at daylight the winds picked up again in earnest, tossing them about in the air like leaves, and creating huge waves below. Only Gabe seemed to enjoy the bumpy ride.

To add to their misery, the heavens opened, and rain poured down. Gabe howled when the cold water hit his face. Logos pulled the sling over Gabe's head to keep him dry, but then the child squirmed and cried because he couldn't see. The rain soon soaked their feathers, increasing the weight they were carrying. They flung their wings downward again and again to shed water.

Tomos motioned them higher, probably hoping to find gentler air, but the winds were even worse aloft, forcing them back down. Logos was afraid the wind might damage Tamara's pods and was on his way over to ask Tomos if they should let some of the air out, when a huge gust blew them downward at the same time as a rogue wave crested and slammed into them. All at once they found themselves floating in the ocean, surrounded by towering waves.

26

DESPERATION

Gabe screamed as the cold water soaked him, and salt water burned his eyes. Tomos and Logos bumped into Tamara and managed to grab her. The forces trying to tear them apart was tremendous. Logos didn't think they could hold her. "I'll hold on to you!" Tomos said. "Rope us to her!"

As the waves tossed them about like driftwood, Tomos held Logos and Tamara while Logos undid their belt cords and tied them both to Tamara. Logos untied a pod from Tamara's harness, let out some of air so the pod would bend, and wound it around her waist for flotation. The other pod he tried to give to Tomos, but Tomos insisted Logos put it on. Logos wiped Gabe's eyes, and his cries died down to whimpers.

The seas pounded them. Every time a wave broke over them, Logos held his breath until his lungs threatened to burst, and he feared they would never surface. But each time, the pods brought them up to the surface. Logos was terrified that Gabe would drown. However, he seemed to know instinctively to hold his breath under water. When they bobbed to the surface again, he screamed his displeasure.

The waves were relentless. Logos had never been so tired, and he didn't know how long he could hold out. He feared for Tamara and Gabe. He felt himself losing consciousness, and wondered idly how it felt to drown. He closed his eyes, but Tomos shook him awake. "Hang on, the storm is dying down," he said. Logos realized that the wind had weakened, and the waves had grown smaller. The moon was peeking out of the clouds. He held Gabe up in the air to shake some of the water off him. Gabe laughed and kicked his legs as though he thought Logos were playing a new game. Logos poured a few drops of fresh water from his carrier into Gabe's mouth.

Tamara said, "I'm almost out of water."

"Me, too," Tomos added.

Logos said, "Let's save what we have for Gabe."

Clouds covered the moon again, and the night seemed endless. To make the time go faster, they told stories. Tomos talked about guard school. Logos told about his trial at Flat Top Mountain, and about what happened the night the tree fell on him. Tomos said that Eckles had gone to the Council and accused him of helping Logos escape, but Tomos had reminded them that since Logos was his rival, he would have loved for him to have been caught and exiled to Flat Top Mountain. The argument had convinced them.

"Father never told me anything about that!" Tamara exclaimed. "Did you help Logos escape?" she asked Tomos.

"I...I." Tomos stuttered.

Tamara turned to Logos. "He did, didn't he? Why didn't you tell me?"

"We didn't want you involved."

"Thank you, Tomos," she said.

Tomos shrugged. "I have a lot of sleep to catch up on."

"At least you won't fall out of the sky," Logos said, chuckling, but Tomos didn't reply. He was already asleep.

Logos and Tamara sang songs and told lame jokes until they started yawning. Logos knew Tamara had fallen asleep when she stopped talking. One of them had to stay awake in case the ropes came untied. He snugged Gabe tighter in his sling and waited for dawn, struggling to stay awake.

When the sun rose, he nudged Tomos. "The sea is calm. We must try to get in the air now, but how? My feathers are completely waterlogged."

"Mine, too," Tomos said, "but if I can get my wings above the surface of the water, I should be able to pull myself out. Let's fully inflate both pods and see how high they'll lift me. I'll need both of them. You'll have to keep Tamara afloat for a while."

Logos seriously doubted if he could do that, but since he had no choice, he nodded. He removed the pod from around his waist and inflated it to its limit. Then he kissed Tamara awake. "We need your pod for awhile," he said. "Tomos is going to try to get out of the water. He'll need both pods, so we'll be on our own until he comes back for us."

Tamara's eyes went wide.

"Don't worry," Logos said, trying to sound more confident than he was, "I'll keep you afloat." Tamara gave a doubtful smile.

Tomos held the newly filled pod while Logos unwound the other pod from Tamara and inflated it. Then Tomos freed himself from the circle. Loosening his belt cord, he pulled the cord up under his shoulders and Logos tied both pods to it.

"The pods are lifting me," Tomos said, kicking his feet, "but it's not enough."

"I'll boost you up," Logos said. He grabbed Tomos by the waist and hoisted him up with all his strength, submerging himself and taking Tamara and Gabe down with him.

Tomos' wings cleared just high enough for him to snap them forward and down, lifting his body out of the water.

One more powerful downstroke, and he was aloft, beating his wings up and down to shed water and showering a cheering Logos and Tamara. Gabe spat out a mouthful of water, and howled.

Without the sky pods, Logos and Tamara fought to keep their heads above water. Logos pulled Gabe from the sling and held him over his head. "Kick your feet!" he ordered Tamara. They kept going under. Just when Logos thought they wouldn't last another moment, Tomos buzzed by. "Untie yourselves!" he shouted.

Logos and Tamara struggled with the wet knots and then they were apart. "Tamara, hold up your arms," Tomos shouted. "Logos, lift her up when I fly by!"

Tamara held up her arms. Tomos circled wide. Flying back at terrific speed, pods trailing out behind him, he grabbed Tamara and hauled her up into the air, water streaming off her body. Logos cheered. Tomos shifted his grip to Tamara's waist and held her out at arms length, facing him. "Snap your wings downward—hard!" he yelled.

Tamara did this, over and over, shedding water with every downstroke. Tomos tied her pods to her, released her to fly, and when she started gaining altitude, he returned for Logos. Logos was heavier, and the first two times, Tomos lost his grip and dropped Logos back into the ocean. On the third attempt, Tomos succeeded, and Logos swung free in the air, shaking water from his wings. They resumed their flight.

The sun soon dried them off and they continued uneventfully for another full day. Although the sun provided plenty of nourishment for energy, they were desperately thirsty. They gave the last of their water to Gabe. Their mouths grew dry and their tongues thick. Talking became an effort, so they lapsed into silence. Without water they would die. Logos now knew for certain that he'd done the wrong thing trying to take Tamara and Gabe across the ocean.

The next morning, the dew was heavy and settled on their wings. They kept flinging the water off, but Gabe started licking the beads of moisture off his sling, and they all followed his example. Logos motioned Tomos over and asked, "If scrape the water off my wings, do you think you can catch some of it in your water carrier?"

"That's the first good idea you've had!" Tomos exclaimed.

They practiced synchronizing their speed and position. "You just hold a constant speed, I'll match my speed to you," Tomos told Logos.

Logos tried his best, but flying at a constant speed with shifting winds was more difficult than he thought. He'd watched the guards flying in formation and they made it look so easy. Without warning, the stunt turned dangerous. They clipped wings, almost sending them into the ocean. They circled and regrouped. "I guess that wasn't such a great idea," Logos said.

"No. It'll work," Tomos insisted. "I forgot you've never flown in formation. Let's try again. Slow down and keep your wings more horizontal when you stop to scrape the water off—like you're gliding. Otherwise, you'll twist in the air."

Logos tried the new flight pattern. "That's better," Tomos said. Now when you see me hold up my water bottle, scrape the water off. Logos did and Tomos succeeded in catching a few drops, and as he perfected his technique, he caught more. Moving to Logos' other side, they repeated the operation.

"You can take my water, too," Tamara said.

"All right," Tomos said, "but I don't want you pausing in the air. Logos, grab hold of her."

Logos flew in front of Tamara and grabbed her. Tomos flew up behind and beneath them, and after some experimentation, matched his wing beats to Logos' keeping his wings as low as possible.

"Now," he told Tamara, holding up his carrier.

Tamara slid her hand down her wing, forcing the water off, and soon Tomos had a full water bottle. They let Gabe drink his fill and then they each took a couple of swallows. Every time the dew reformed on their wings, they repeated the procedure until all their containers were full.

The air and sea continued calm. Another day and night went by without any major incidents, although Logos knew they didn't cover as much distance as before, and they always needed more water than they had. On the following morning, gulls appeared. Tomos wanted to fly higher to look for land, but Logos dissuaded him, successfully arguing that he needed to save his energy. Logos prayed they were close to land. He didn't think they could go much farther. The pods were leaking badly and were half their size. They were afraid to try to reinflate them, lest they burst. He strained his eyes, hoping to see anything green—anything living. They must be close to land.

His hopes were dashed when a fog bank descended from nowhere. One moment everything was fine, and the next, a giant cloud enclosed them. "Stay close to me," Tomos ordered.

Once again, they relied on Tomos' keen ears to maintain their altitude. But now when the fog condensed on their wings, visibility was too poor to collect water safely. They licked off what they could reach and flung off the rest of the precious water.

Eventually Tamara's pods lost so much loft they had no choice but to try to reinflate them. Tomos was carrying Tamara. One pod had just been inflated and reattached. Logos was inflating the other one. Without warning, the pod attached to Tamara popped open and collapsed, swinging Tomos and Tamara sideways and dropping them dangerously near the water. Tomos compensated with powerful downstrokes, and managed to stay in the air, but then the pod smacked into the water, pulling them down, and he and Tamara were floating in the ocean again. Logos circled above helplessly, watching Tomos and Tamara struggle to hold onto each other and disconnect the pod.

Tomos detached the burst pod and let go of it. It started to drift off.

"No, keep it!" Tamara said. "Maybe I can repair it."

Tomos grabbed the pod and wrapped it around her waist. Logos flew closer. "I'll get you out!" he shouted. "Grab this pod next time I fly by."

"Be careful!" Tomas shouted. "Time the waves, and keep your wings up—don't get too close to the water!"

Logos flew by holding out the fully inflated pod. Tomos lunged for it and missed. On the third pass, Tomos grabbed it. "I'll need this to get out," he told Tamara as he attached the filled pod to his belt. "You'll have to manage on your own for a while. Tamara's eyes went wide. "Kick your legs and move your arms," Tomos said. "Ready!" he shouted to Logos, letting go of Tamara and lifting his arms.

Logos flew by, grabbed Tomos and tried to snatch the heavy sylvan out of the water, but he was unable to lift him high enough for him to clear his wings, and he almost fell in himself. He recovered, and they tried again with Tamara giving Tomos a feeble boost, but they failed again.

"You're just wasting your energy," Tomos yelled at Logos, "Take Tamara instead."

"I'll get in the water and boost you up," Logos yelled.

"No!" Tomos shouted. "I can't get out with one pod. You must get Tamara out!" He switched the good pod to Tamara. "On three," he shouted at Logos.

"Logos circled wide and dived back at high speed. Tomos watched Logos' flight path and gauged his speed.

"One-two-three!" Tomos yelled. On three, he lifted Tamara above his head, Logos grabbed her hands and pulled her into the air. He struggled to gain altitude, then tossed her into the air and grabbed her by the waist. She started throwing off water off her wings.

"Good job!" Tomos yelled when he popped back up to the surface and saw they were in the air.

Logos circled back. "As soon as Tamara dries off, we'll get you out."

"No!" Tomos yelled, "It's too dangerous, and it won't work. I'm too heavy. Don't waste your strength. Leave me and keep going. We have to be close to land now."

"We can't just abandon you," Logos shouted.

"I'll be all right. Go!" Tomos thundered.

Logos turned and set a course for the west. As he carried Tamara higher in the sky, fog settled over Tomos, closing him off from sight.

Near exhaustion and sick at heart, Logos flew on, trying to gauge his distance from the sound and smell of the ocean as Tomos had taught him. The fog condensed on their wings again, making them heavier. They both kept flinging the water off. Tamara with only one pod, looked exhausted. Logos could only carry her for brief spells, before getting winded. They were at the end of their strength, and he wondered how much farther they would be able to continue. He cursed himself for putting Tamara and Gabe in such danger.

The remaining pod was shrinking rapidly, but Logos didn't dare add air. If the last pod split, they were finished. Tamara was losing altitude, so Logos picked her up again. She put her hands around his neck and laid her head on his shoulder. Gabe smiled and grabbed a handful of her hair. She cupped his little head in her hand.

"Tamara, I'm sorry I got you into this …," Logos began.

She stopped him. "We both knew the risk. If we fall in the ocean again, let's tie the pod to Gabe and release him. Maybe the wind will carry him to land, and some kind human will find him. At least he'll have a chance."

Unable to speak, Logos kissed her forehead and flew on in the enveloping whiteness, praying the fog would life and wondering what had happened to Tomos.

All at once Tamara said, "The air smells different. Can't you smell it?"

Logos took a deep breath. The air *did* smell different. It smelled of seaweed, seashells, wet sand and …pine needles. "We're near land," he said, his voice raising with excitement. He strained to listen. "I can't hear the waves anymore. " A short time later he asked, "Do you feel that?"

"What?"

"Warm air. I think maybe we're over trees."

Lessening his speed, Logos glided lower, keeping an ear tuned to the sound. Then the fog thinned for a moment, and below them, he made out a forest. "Land!" he exclaimed.

Tamara cheered.

Circling back the way they came, they returned to the ocean. Logos landed on a white, sandy beach, and his knees collapsed, dumping them all on the sand. Tamara said, "I never thought I'd be this happy to be on the ground." They threw themselves into each other's arms and fell into an exhausted sleep.

***

Logos awoke when something sharp hit his face. He sat up. Gabe had wiggled out of the sling and was playing in the sand. Gabe saw him sit up, giggled and threw another fistful of sand in Logos' direction. Logos looked around him. The sun had burned the fog away and filled his wings with new energy. Gentle waves were lapping on the beach. He didn't know how long he had slept.

"Come here, you little miscreant," Logos said, picking up Gabe and tucking him back in his sling. He kissed Tamara awake. "Get up. The fog's lifted. I've got to search for Tomos. You stay here and rest and sun."

From above, he saw only the forest and the unbroken band of white sand stretching in both directions as far as he could see. He flew in one direction, then the other until he tired and had to land to rest. Then just when he was about to give up and turn back, he spotted a dark object lying on the shore. Fearful of what he might find, he landed, but it turned out to be only a half-waterlogged tree that had washed up on the beach. He flew back to Tamara. "I hate to stop searching for Tomos, but I've got to go find some fresh water," he said.

He flew inland where he found a chain of lakes of sparkling clear water. He saw no sign of human occupation, so he landed and filled both their water bottles. He returned to Tamara and sat down with her and Gabe.

"Did you see any tall trees?" she asked.

Logos shook his head. "I hate to disappoint you, but I didn't see a one. There's this great forest of huge trees, some of them pretty tall, but no silkiron trees. This is a beautiful, unspoiled land—nothing but trees and rivers and lakes as far as the eye can see—like what we're told our country used to be before humans took over."

"Did you go all the way to the other coast?"

"No." He paused. "It must be farther than we think. We may need the sky pods again."

"See any humans?"

"No, thank the Goddess!"

Gabe lay down and waved his arms through the sand.

Tamara picked him up and brushed him off. "Look what you did," she said. "You made a little sylvan—or is it one of the Benefield angels? Gabe laughed and clapped his hands as though he understood.

Logos smiled. "You stay here with him. I'm going to search for Tomos again."

He flew up the coast for two mehlas, returned to Tamara, and then few down the coast in the other direction. He flew until the sun sank into the Goddess' bower, when he again returned to Tamara. They needed to find shelter before nightfall.

Her face fell when he returned alone. "Nothing?"

"No sign of him. Surely if he made it, I would've found him by now—or he would've found us. We have to assume the worst—that he's drowned."

Tamara began to weep. "Oh, poor Tomos. We never would have made it without him. He saved our lives."

"Yes, he did, several times, and he sacrificed himself for us, but I'll search again tomorrow. If we can find his body, at least we can give him a proper funeral."

Tamara burst into sobs.

That night they took refuge in the top fork of a pine tree, Gabe tucked securely in Logos' vest so he couldn't wriggle out. The next morning, when Logos announced he was going out to search for Tomos, Tamara said, Give me your belt cord. While you're gone I'll repair the sky pods."

"That's a good idea. We'll need them again." Tomos said as he pulled the cord off his waist and handed it to her.

That day and the next, Logos found nothing. When he came back alone the third day, he said, "I hate to say this, but I think we should abandon the search and move on. We don't know how far it is to the far shore or what the weather is like there. We need to go and get settled."

Tears ran down Tamara's face. "I was counting on Tomos to return to New Solari and tell my parents that I'm okay. Now they'll never know."

"You know that he probably would have been exiled for helping us escape?

"You're right. Perhaps we could have talked him into going with us." She glanced at the deserted beaches and the endless ocean and shivered. "We're completely alone here."

Logos turned her chin to face him and wiped away her tears with his thumbs. "We have each other—and a son. That's a family."

She smiled and nestled into his arms

Logos looked over her head into the gathering darkness. "Tomorrow at dawn, we leave to find the Goddess' Grove."

"Do you really think it exists?" Tamara asked.

"Definitely, and you and I will find it and make a new home."

THE END

NOTE FROM THE AUTHOR

Thank you for buying my book. Like most independent authors, my only advertising comes from word of mouth and reviews. Please recommend my book to your friends and family. If you could take a minute to leave a review for *Malvan Born* on Amazon.com, it would be extremely helpful

My other novels:

The History of the Malvans: For young adults. Available on Amazon.com as a printed book. (This is the prequel to Malvan Born): The incredible story of how the malvans were born, how they changed sylvan society, and the problems both races faced when humans came along.

The Mystery of the Green Spider: A Zepp Jones Adventure. For grades 3 through 6. Available on Amazon.com as an ebook and a printed book.

Two elementary schools compete for prizes (including a lightning-fast computer) in a science project competition. When fifth graders Zepp Jones and his best friend, Matt, decide to study the life cycle of spiders, all goes well until their spider does something completely unexpected which could very well get them disqualified from the competition.

***Prairie Hopes*:*: For grades 3 through 6. Available on Amazon.com as an ebook and a printed book.

When polio strikes Todd Wright's family, his father can't walk, and his mother loses touch with reality. Todd, 11, suddenly finds himself in charge.

A kindly doctor makes arrangements to place the whole family in institutions. Todd promises his little sister, Jenny, 7, that she'll never have to go to an orphanage, but worries that he won't be able to keep his promise.

If only their mother would come to her senses, they might be able to manage. As time draws near for them to leave, Todd and Jenny redouble their efforts to reach her.

Visit my website:

www. LimberlostBooks.com

for more information on my books.

www.ingramcontent.com/pod-product-compliance
Lightning Source LLC
Chambersburg PA
CBHW070619130626
46556CB00001B/414